Hanged for a Sheep

Also by Rosemary Gatenby

DEADLY RELATIONS

AIM TO KILL

EVIL IS AS EVIL DOES

Hanged for a Sheep

ROSEMARY GATENBY

A Red Badge Novel of Suspense

DODD, MEAD & COMPANY
NEW YORK

ISBN: 0-396-06712-3
Library of Congress Catalog Card Number: 72-6883
Printed in the United States of America
by Vail-Ballou Press, Inc., Binghamton, N.Y.

For Mamie

1722974

The town of Selkirk, in this book, is entirely fictional. Its faults could as well be found anywhere else in the country, and were in no way suggested by acquaintanceship with the nice, friendly small towns of my native state. Actually I picked the locale for reasons of nostalgia.

The characters are of course also completely imaginary.

R. G.

Chapter 1

SELKIRK, INDIANA, is a pleasant enough little town, supported by three factories, a cannery, and the farms which stretch flatly away on all sides, dotted with pigs, spotted with cows, and squared off into fields that yearly produce nothing but bumper crops.

It's a comfortable town. Friendly. People entertain a great deal there, and though the number of bridge hands dealt by the ladies in an average week has never been estimated, it must be formidable. Rotary, Kiwanis, and the Lions Club loom large.

Gilman and Enid Weir had lived in Selkirk all their married lives—Gil having, at the completion of his education, returned with a bride and a law degree to hang out his shingle (as they still say there) in the old home town.

Until the autumn when everything fell to pieces for Gil Weir, his and Enid's marriage had seemed, to most people in town, to be perfectly solid, averagely happy. The one exception to this common belief in the connubial contentment of the Weirs was in the mind of a young woman named Henrietta Fitchly. Henrietta was the best friend of Barbara Dresser, Gilman Weir's secretary. And Henrietta alone had been entrusted, over a period of perhaps two years, with one little bauble of information after another, by now amounting to an Add-A-Pearl necklace of some size.

Barbara had not meant, originally, to say so much. She had been driven, first by Henrietta's bragging about her rich boyfriend from Indianapolis, and second by her own need to appear (to someone at least) to be desirable to men even in the face of the evidence that none had asked her out in the last three years.

"If only Gil weren't married, of course . . ." was all she said to begin with, lowering her velvety brown eyes discreetly and touching a hand to the knot of hair at the nape of her neck. She was a rather plain girl. Though plainness was not her problem. Her problem was that she was shy and stand-offish. The impression she gave men was that if advances were to be made, these would be promptly rebuffed—a guess that would have been wrong. But the matter had never been put to the test; if it had, Barbara Dresser would have become Barbara Something-else and not a vessel of frustration, discontent, and partially sublimated lust.

His secretary's sexual qualifications, or lack of them, were a matter that had never even crossed Gil Weir's mind as worthy of any speculation about—other than a purely automatic and absolutely objective glance at her legs from time to time. Barbara was part of the accouterment of his office and of little more interest to him than her electric typewriter or his dictating machine.

In accordance with popular belief about it, then, Gil Weir's twenty-year marriage to Enid was quite happy, right up to and including part of that August. Especially happy since he and Enid had become parents. There had been a period, before Maggie, when Enid Weir had become rather neurotic; her inability to produce a child had caused her to blame herself for saddling Gil with a barren wife, and brought on periods of hysterical crying. But that was long over with. The adoption of little Margaret twelve years ago had turned out to be most felicitous.

"Of course Enid's terribly possessive," Barbara Dresser told her friend Henrietta. "Always keeping an eye on him."

"Well, you can see why—wouldn't *you?*"

"What do you mean, exactly, Henrietta?" Barbara was

wondering just how much her friend had read into some of the inferences she'd made; if Henrietta, in the light of her own experience, assumed that Barbara was really having an affair with Gil Weir, that was certainly not anything she had ever actually been told.

"Well, I mean—isn't she older than Gil?"

Barbara frowned—a shade disappointed that they were not, after all, directly discussing her own relationship to her employer. "Older? Not much, I think. Some women just age rapidly. Hit their forties and fall apart. Menopause."

As a matter of fact Gil Weir was forty-four and Enid was forty-six.

"I suppose she may have been rather attractive when she was young." (Barbara to Henrietta over a Coke and a sandwich at lunch.) "But for Gil to be tied to her now . . ."

"Bad luck, isn't it?" (For Barbara, her luncheon companion meant.) "The good ones just always seem to be married." Worse than a sore point with Henrietta; her own miscalculations about her married boyfriend's intention of divorcing his wife had stranded her last year, high and dry, and very single at an age by which all the local fellows had long since settled down to raise a family.

The trouble that finally worked its way up to such an unexpected climax began in early August at the dedication of the new wing which had been added to the Selkirk Public Library.

"I *have* to go?" Gil asked. "You know that with the time we're teeing off Sunday—"

"You'll just have to tee off earlier or not at all." Enid could be gallingly determined in someone else's behalf. "The Library Board are disappointed enough that your mother can't be here. And after all the years she served on the board . . ."

His mother had generously (or to his mind, foolishly—

she couldn't afford it) given the money for a new circulation desk; and now she wasn't well enough to come up from Florida for the dedication.

"They'll expect you to be there in her place, Gil, and the news photographers will cover the ceremony I'm sure, and if I'm not able to send your mother a picture from the *News* showing you and the desk—"

"O.K., O.K., I'll be there."

And so it was that he found himself all dressed in shirt and tie and a suit—unheard of for him on a summer Sunday—perspiring in the new library wing, for the air conditioning had something wrong with it that they had been unable to fix in time for the festivities.

On close inspection he could see why, after all, the desk had cost so much. (Four thousand dollars.) It was big. Made of beautiful wood, and with complicated innards.

The sticky, non-alcoholic punch was making him thirstier than ever as he stood conversing with the new head of the library—a man, surprisingly, who would replace Mrs. Semple now that she was retiring. Name of Sidney Strait. With a bone-crunching handshake—something to make up for being such a little fellow—he'd said to call him Sid.

Sid had progressed from his kind, if fulsome remarks about Gil's mother's gift to other things. "The per volume investment—which is not, you know, oriented—" (What was he talking about?)

But thank God here came Mrs. Semple, Strait's predecessor as library head, with Enid in tow. Now he could phase out the duty conversation and go talk to someone of his own choosing.

"I didn't realize, Enid, that you hadn't met our Mr. Strait." The about-to-retire head librarian's timeless face (it *must* be timeless, because Gil remembered Mrs. Semple's looking exactly the same when she'd been in charge of the Children's Department thirty-five years ago; of course he'd thought then that she was old, but she couldn't have been

—not by his present standard of "old"), a paper-pale face bounded on three sides by short reddish hair and individualized by the worst set of large, crooked buck teeth he had ever seen, appeared beside him, turning to him with a momentary "Hello, Gil," and back to Mr. Strait, with a toothful though not toothsome smile: "I've been working so closely with Sidney since he came, it's as if he'd already been here in Selkirk for years."

Gil moved back a pace to make room for Enid and for two people standing behind him, who apparently intended to join their conversation, being probably tired of their own —Ruth and Hugh Commiger, as worthwhile and tiresome a couple as you could find in a month of Sundays, as the saying goes, let alone this particular Sunday.

"Enid—" Mrs. Semple smiled across the intervening Commigers. "Enid, this is Sidney Strait. Sidney, this is Mrs. Weir."

Sidney Strait leaned forward from the waist and took Enid's hand in his strong grip. Gil sympathized; he could almost hear the bones grinding together, and indeed a small grimace of pain was stillborn in his wife's face. "Mrs. Weir! This is certainly a pleasure." Sidney's eyes, looking unnaturally large through the thick lenses of his glasses, emphasized the sincerity of the feeling he expressed. "I've looked forward *so* much to meeting you! Your so very generous gift to the library, of the circulation desk—"

For a moment Enid's face was a trifle blank. Then as she realized the man's error, she broke in. "But it wasn't I who gave—"

Sidney Strait had turned to Gil and so did not notice that Enid had started to say something. "As I was telling your son, Mrs. Weir, the library is *magnificently* in your debt!"

His ringing thanks fell on stunned silence.

Monday morning Enid Weir wished that she didn't have to get up; didn't have to get up ever again, and go out to

5

the grocery, to the cleaners, and to the drugstore, where she would see people, and—God, it was Monday, wasn't it!—to the country club to take Maggie for swim-team practice, where she would undoubtedly be faced by a gaggle of poolside mothers, all of whom had either just heard, or just passed on to someone else, the details of yesterday's contretemps at the library dedication reception.

I'll be the laughingstock of the whole town . . .

She got up and went into the bathroom, where she stood before the mirror and unwisely looked at herself. Never a good idea this soon after waking: the wrinkles that would smooth out later in the day were creased into her skin; her eyes, still slitted with sleep, seemed even smaller than they were (piglike?) and certainly duller; and her hair, uncombed, stood out every which way, like Medusa's snakes.

It was appallingly gray. Her hair.

She hadn't known it was *that* gray, and realized that she hadn't looked at it critically in a long time. She had, actually, been feeling quite superior to friends who had had their locks frosted: all so alike, all so fake-looking.

Well, hers was real—the gray. Every bit of it. *As I was telling your son, Mrs. Weir—*

Of course Gil was one of those boyish-looking men who never aged. And not a hair on his head had turned. It was the boyishness, the look of needing to be mothered and taken care of, that had appealed to her most, she supposed, when they had met twenty-two years ago at a lecture at Columbia University. A charm that still worked.

For the first time—well, for the first time since yesterday—she seriously asked herself whether her husband continued to find her physically attractive. How? How, when he saw her every morning without her makeup, as she was seeing herself this minute?

Maybe, like Enid herself, he had failed to notice? Ah, no. After the scene yesterday he would surely have taken stock. Had the scales fallen from his eyes, had he been shocked, to

6

see for himself that he was married to a woman in declining middle age?

She stooped over to take the bathmat off the side of the tub, over which it was draped, and laid it on the floor, preparatory to taking a shower.

In this position, when she was leaning far over, the bags under her eyes hung down so that she could actually see them.

She could have cried.

Yet this crisis might have blown over. Enid waited ten days—she didn't want anyone to suppose she'd been frightened into it by the library episode—and then got her hair colored. She didn't like the way it turned out, but quite a number of her friends told her it looked wonderful, and she tried to believe it.

The thing that further upset her, so that Sidney Strait's words instead of fading from her mind as the days passed acquired in memory an ever more significant and perhaps sinister quality, like the handwriting on the wall, was the Fred Towse affair.

"Have you heard anything about Fred Towse?" she asked Gil when he came home for lunch the day Beth Towse told her about it.

"Fred?" They stood in the coolness of the vestibule with its red-tiled floor and gold, buff, brown and rust striped wallpaper. "Why? Did he get a promotion or something?" He was aware that Fred had been hoping for some time for substantial advancement.

"He hasn't said anything to you about meeting this girl . . . ?"

"What girl?"

"Well, if he told you to keep quiet about her, you don't have to anymore, because Beth knows, and she told me this morning. The reason Beth knows is because he wants a divorce."

"A divorce? Fred?" He was staring at her, incredulous.

"A divorce. Fred. It seems nice, sweet, innocent-looking Fred has been having an affair with some girl in Terre Haute. Some girl in a customer's office, where he goes regularly on business. Three *years* Beth says this has been going on, and she never had a suspicion! Only now, he wants to marry her. The girl."

"I don't believe it. Fred?" He shook his head and walked on into the living room, to stand lost in thought in the center of the textured beige carpeting. "He's just not the philandering type!"

"And it's not as if Beth had given him cause."

"He must have flipped his lid." (Gil was always adopting what he thought was current slang when it was no longer current.)

How had Fred deceived everyone so completely? Enid wondered. She remembered clearly the last time they'd had dinner at the Towses'; how affectionate he had been with the poor deluded girl, the mother of his children. Deliberately, no doubt, to allay suspicion. He had looked just as usual, as nice, as guileless as Gil did this minute. How wicked.

Thoughtfully, after lunch, with the Towse drama still going through her mind like an episode from daytime T.V., she watched Gil open the mail.

"What's funny?" she asked; he was looking at a bill.

"Funny? Oh, I was just thinking about Fred. The old goat!"

She stiffened. "That's *funny?*"

The smile faded under her disapproval. "Of course it's not funny, actually. I—"

"Tragic is more like it."

"Well, sad. Certainly very sad to see a marriage break up. And the kids and all."

"And Beth. Don't you like Beth? You think she's finding all this funny? Amusing?"

"Of *course* I like Beth. I feel damn sorry about it. What I was laughing at was Fred. Pulling a fast one like that. Three years? And no one suspecting . . ."

"You sound as if you envy him!"

"Hey!" He leaned over and pecked her passionlessly on the cheek. "Don't get so mad! Envy him? Not me. O.K., I shouldn't have laughed. But you don't understand. It's just a male reaction, that's all. Nothing to do with my personal feelings about the Towses. Locker-room humor, I guess."

Yes, indeed! thought Enid. The things that men thought funny . . . All sex-oriented, weren't they. And there probably wouldn't be a husband in town who didn't envy Fred Towse. Just as Gil did . . . That didn't wish *they* were in Fred's shoes . . . Just as Gil did . . . ?

She sat, later that same afternoon, in her sister's kitchen, in the Strothers house a few blocks from her own—an ugly, old Dutch Colonial house which had seemingly been built without a floor plan, ending up a maze of small, dark rooms and purposeless hallways with all sorts of doors opening off them and into each other.

"No, you just never know." Enid's sister Phyllis echoed her own words. "*I* didn't."

Phyllis's husband had deserted her. Had run away with the farm girl they'd had living with them to help take care of the children when the fourth baby had been born. Beejay—as he'd been known to everyone in Selkirk all his life —had fled to California with Darlene, thence never to return. Phyll had divorced him, of course, and had surprisingly stayed on in what had been Beejay's home town. Enjoying, perhaps, her role of martyr? "So brave, that girl! Knuckling right down and getting a job to support herself, bringing up those four children all alone." If she had gone back to Akron, whence she had come, she'd have been just another divorcee saddled with a pack of offspring, struggling to make her way. ("Her marriage failed, you know.")

It had been on a visit to her newly married sister that

Phyllis had met Beejay Strothers. And so it was Enid she had to thank—if that was the word—for her being in Selkirk in the first place. Though it was certainly her own doing to have married and stayed.

Phyll worked in the Merchants National Bank. Had for ten years. Her eldest, Marilyn, (eighteen) was in college, and her second child and oldest son, Benson, (just graduated from high school at seventeen) was in a pet because he couldn't afford to go. ("Mom's sending *her, Marilyn,* a *girl,* to college! *Why?* She'll just get married, she doesn't *need* a college education. What in the world does Mom expect *me* to do, work as a peeler at the canning factory?") Joyce would be a ninth-grader when school started this fall, and Bobby, who was indirectly responsible for their fatherless condition because it was with him that Phyll Strothers had been occupied at the time of Beejay's infatuation and subsequent defection, was ten.

Phyll, having because of circumstances taken a dislike to men, was spearheading the Women's Lib movement in town.

So she was perfectly happy to be able to say a few unkind words about Fred Towse.

"No, you really just don't ever know." And she launched into a full-bodied, many-hued recounting of the news she'd just received of a divorce impending back in Akron.

"It's that dangerous age. That men get to. Enid, I don't like your hair. It looks dyed."

"It's *not* dyed. It's a rinse. Lasts a month."

"Well, be thankful it's not permanent." Phyll ran a hand over her own perfectly executed coiffure, dark as a raven's wing with no artificial assistance. "Can't you try a different color next time?"

"Oh. Well, I suppose so."

"This one makes your skin look old. Leached out."

"Oh."

She should be grateful to Phyll for telling her. Your best friend never would; too tactful. But tact made life more pleasant—didn't it?

"I hope you *really* keep your eye on that secretary of Gil's—you do, don't you, Enid?"

"Barbara? Oh, she's all right. A nice girl, kind of quiet—"

"They often are. Mousy, even, some of these home-wreckers; make a man feel big and important, the way they hang on every word. *I* wouldn't be so complacent, if my husband were closeted every day with some girl with a figure like Barbara Dresser's—did you ever really analyze what she's got under those tweedy things she wears, and those high-necked blouses? Not bad."

It was on the tip of Enid's tongue to say that it wasn't Phyll's husband closeted with Barbara Dresser, seeing as hers had already flown the coop. But she let it go.

And the next time she was in Gil's office she did take a quick survey of little Miss Dresser's figure—and came away unhappy. Those big brown eyes, too . . . Somehow Phyll's warnings about her combined in Enid's mind with the girl's innocuous appearance to form what could only be termed a discrepancy. The impression Enid carried away with her that day—down the stairs from the second-floor office and along the street to her car, standing at an expired parking meter and with a ticket on its windshield (oh, no! not my day, today!)—was that Barbara was to all intents and purposes lying; she was not what she seemed to be.

Chapter 2

GIL HARDLY knew his wife these days. She couldn't always have been like this and he just hadn't noticed? Maybe it was some kind of menopausal trauma . . . or she was mentally ill? She seemed to have something like, well, delusions.

Always cross-questioning him about his days. Checking up on him.

And she seemed almost to hold him personally responsible for the breakup of the Towses' marriage. Simply because he was still speaking to Fred.

Fred had slunk into his office one day—almost furtively.

"Just say the word and I won't even sit down. I may already have damaged your reputation merely by coming here."

"Relax, Fred!" He nodded at the leather easy chair by the desk. How haggard Fred looked . . .

"If you're still speaking to me, you're the only one in town who is." Fred took out a cigarette and lit it. "Beth got to everyone first, you know. I've been painted as a horny monster with—"

"Well, aren't you?" Gil shoved the ashtray over for him.

"Yeah, I guess so. Well, Beth can have this town, I'm getting out. She can keep the friends—I've lost them. Except you, I guess? Patty and I are going to start over. In Danville."

"Danville. Is that the promotion you've been—"

Fred's eyes didn't quite meet his. "Not a promotion. No. Lateral move—the company has another office there. I'm dead in *this* territory, obviously."

"Fred, aren't you—jumping into this without thinking it through? Beth's a helluva nice girl, and I can't see—"

"No one ever does see, from the outside. Since *grade school;* grade school that Beth first got her hooks in me. I've tried. I've tried, God help me, to measure up to what she expected of me. But we were a misfit. A total misfit."

"A misfit? You and Beth?" They had appeared to be the perfect match.

"With Patty I'm a new person. It's a revelation, Gil. A revelation. I didn't know what I was capable of till I met that girl!" The last time Gil had seen a look like that on anyone's face, it had been worn by a friend who was about to make his first million on a stock-market tip. (He had, instead, lost his shirt.)

"It's going to cost you more than you think—"

"Worth it." Fred took a last puff of his cigarette and ground it out in the ashtray. The very picture of the friendly, clean-cut, nice-looking Midwestern American male who does not look his age of forty-five; he'd always reminded Gil of Dick Foran, in the movies. Oh, today he looked his age, maybe, but that was the worry he'd been going through, juggling a wife and a girlfriend.

"I'm not asking you to represent me in the divorce. You'd be run out of town on a rail, I imagine. But will you represent Beth?"

"If she wants me to. And if I do, I warn you, I'll take you for every nickel we can get."

But Fred could no more be dissuaded from leaving his wife for Patty who-was-twenty-eight than you could talk a crazed miner out of gold fever.

Beth did not retain him as her lawyer; instead, she took his advice, which was to get a lawyer from Indianapolis, one who specialized in divorce cases and who would get a better settlement for her, Gil said, than he would.

Enid construed this development according to her own

ideas of the situation.

"You didn't *want* to represent Beth. In spite of all Fred's done, and of all you've said about disapproving of this—this affair of his, I do believe you still consider Fred Towse a friend of yours!"

"Well, certainly I do. I never slammed the door in his face because he voted Democrat, either. His politics and his morals are his affair, not mine."

"What a way to put it! Infidelity means no more to you than the difference between voting row A or row B on the voting machine?"

That had been some argument . . .

And he had agreed, after all, to represent Fred. "No one," his friend pointed out, "can blame you now for handling my case. Not when Beth had her pick first—you or the out-of-town smart-ass."

It was just as Enid had thought, she told him. He'd been on Fred's side all along.

And Gil felt saddened—saddened and older, as change makes us all feel older—when his best friend packed up, and moved from the local motel to bachelor digs in Danville, down near Indianapolis.

"I hear your brother-in-law's handling Fred Towse's side of the divorce for him," Ernestine Fitchly (Henrietta Fitchly's mother) said to Phyllis Strothers as she handed her an endorsed dividend check and a deposit slip through the narrow teller's window.

"Yes, I believe he is."

"I wouldn't think that would sit very well with your sister. Beth Towse being her best friend. Certainly surprised me."

"Oh, Gil offered to act in Beth's behalf. But he told her she'd be better off with a lawyer who specializes in divorce actions."

"Oh, I see. That was his advice, then."

Ernestine Fitchly sat on the hospital board, ran the United Fund, and wielded enormous power in the Women's Organization of the Presbyterian Church. And she considered the moral tone of Selkirk to be something for which she was personally responsible.

"One wonders, you know," she continued to Phyllis Strothers, tucking the little green deposit receipt away in her suitcase-size handbag, "when to say something. And when not. Gil Weir, it seems to me, is another one that bears watching." Her bright blue eyes, beneath the faded gray eyebrows, fixed upon Phyllis's, alert for some glint of matching suspicion.

Phyll's eyes told nothing. But she leaned momentarily against the counter—a pause in her work rhythm—in expectation of perhaps learning something. "Why do you say that, Mrs. Fitchly?"

Ernestine Fitchly glanced carefully about, for she did not believe in idly spreading gossip. "My daughter tells me—and this is not to be repeated, Phyllis—that something is going on between Gil Weir and Barbara Dresser. Has been for some time. Just how much, I couldn't say—"

"O.K., what is it?" Gil asked as he heard the door of Maggie's room click shut upon his daughter and her record player. "You've been ticking like a time bomb ever since I got home tonight."

Enid was huddled in a chair in the living room, picking at a hangnail. Her lips were pursed together and she was frowning. All through dinner she had seemed to be on the edge of some kind of hysterical outbreak. Her responses to Maggie's conversation—smiles, little laughs, surprise—had been given in jerks, as though she were a puppet with someone pulling abruptly first on these strings, then on those, and quickly letting them go.

15

"Well, something's bothering you," he prompted her, as she still said nothing.

She looked up then. "I have it on very good authority that you're having an affair with Barbara Dresser."

"You *what?* With Barbara? You're out of your mind!"

"I am not. I didn't make it up." Her voice was trembling. "I heard it. On good authority."

"Whose authority? Just tell me that!" He had gotten out of his chair and stood, hands on hips, staring down at his wife.

"Of course I won't tell you. But someone who should know."

Distractedly he ran his hand through his hair and flopped down again into his chair.

"How can anyone know? There's nothing to know! *Nothing!*"

Tremulously, her mouth quirked up. "You wouldn't protest so vehemently if there weren't something to it."

"I *wouldn't?* A totally unexpected and unprovoked accusation—and untrue—and you expect me not to react?"

"If there were nothing to it, you'd have laughed it off."

"You think I would? Last time I laughed at something like that—it was Fred's alleged adultery, that time—you gave me hell."

He got up and started pacing. "Out of a clear blue sky. Tell me—just tell me—where I did what with Barbara Dresser? . . . Did you get it fourth hand? Fifth? You know gossip in this town . . ."

It was useless.

Enid went to bed that night—her bed, the left-hand twin —wearing her martyrdom like a poultice.

Life became harrowing. Gil never knew, when he came home, whether he was going to be given the silent treatment or a painfully contrived attempt at normalcy. In fact Enid herself never knew, in advance; she did what she felt capable of at the time.

She kept hoping for proof that Ernestine Fitchly's story was wrong. But her inability to seize on even a shred of evidence was really, to her mind, an indication of the lengths to which Gil must be going? to conceal his extramarital activities?

Her almost daily sessions with poor dear Beth Towse had of course opened her eyes to much that she had supposed happened only to other people. It was almost like taking a course in the psychology of the middle-aged male. "The over-forty syndrome," Beth called it.

Enid's mirror was one of the most depressing arguments around. Every time she looked into it, she could see for herself that her husband couldn't possibly still find her attractive. What else was she to think, in an America dedicated to and brainwashed by the youth-cult, the beauty-cult, the sex-cult? *I was telling your son, Mrs. Weir . . .*

It was on a day near the end of August that Gil, standing on the corner of Main Street and Pershing, waiting for the light to change, looked across to the opposite corner and did a double take.

If he didn't know better, he'd think that was Cinny Neiswanner. Cinny Howland, rather . . . A tall, broad-shouldered, wide-mouthed blonde, with hair swept back and to one side and caught in a clip, as Cinny had worn hers in high school.

The light changed and the tall blonde stepped down off the curb, came toward him across the street with leggy, athletic grace. Her glance met his, went past him. And then she checked, abruptly, detaching herself from the stream of pedestrians.

"Gil! Gil Weir!" The same amber eyes, matching her hair.

"I thought it couldn't be! How are you, Cinny?"

"Fine. Just fine, Gil—"

His smile faded as he thought of Ted. Must be a couple of years now since Ted Howland had died, leaving Cinny widowed. In New York, where they had lived ever since they'd been married.

"I was so sorry, Cinny. About Ted. It was in the papers here, of course. How have things been going, since?"

Her chin came forward a little, and for a moment she pressed her lips together, as though she were trying to think of an answer that would cover the situation. Then she sort of smiled.

"Oh, it's not so bad as it was at first. I hope things'll be a lot better now, in fact. I've decided to try it here, see if it works out O.K. New York City is no place to raise a child."

"I'm sure you're right about that! So you're back in Selkirk to stay . . ."

"Well, on a trial basis. I've been away so long, you know. And I'll have to see how Trina likes it. My daughter. For the time being we're staying with Ted's aunt—Aunt Lucille?"

"Oh, yes. Miss Howland."

"She's got that immense house, and nobody in it but her—"

It was on the tip of Gil's tongue to say, you and your daughter must come over, when he realized that that would never do. Any such suggestion must come from Enid; and probably never would. She had no doubt heard, when she'd come to Selkirk a bride, that Gil and a girl named Cynthia Neiswanner had at one time been a very steady item. Even if Enid had forgotten, someone would be sure, now that Cinny was back in town, to remind her.

And so he wished Ted's widow good luck and went on his way, feeling as if he had, for a few minutes anyway, shed twenty years.

She had hardly changed. Oh, a more sharply defined jaw line, and he had noticed the crow's-feet etched lightly in at the corners of her eyes when she smiled. More assurance, a becoming maturity, in her manner. But actually, it had seemed almost as if he'd seen her yesterday—or last week.

It had been a very black day, the one on which he'd received her letter. The letter telling him she was engaged to Ted. But with a year and a half yet at Kenyon and three years of law school ahead of him—God, he'd never thought of marriage at that stage of things except as something in the far-distant future.

He'd sent her his blessing and had gone out and gotten very drunk.

But it certainly took him back—seeing her now.

He made no mention of the meeting to Enid—afraid she would misconstrue his eagerness to tell her about it. Let her find out from someone else that his old girlfriend was in town; and he prepared himself to be sufficiently casual when the occasion should arise.

They sat at supper, on the first day of school—Maggie wearing, still, the new jumper and blouse in which she'd attended classes.

"My goodness, seventh grade now, isn't it," Gil said. Maggie was changing, growing up. Such a warm, protective feeling came over Gil as his eyes lingered on the thin little figure, just beginning to show the promise of future development, and on the matchstick arms, which he knew were deceptively strong. Thin, but healthy; she would fill out later. Like all the Weirs. Dark hair, shoulder length, curling delicately about the tan face with its startling, long-lashed blue eyes. And the Weir nose, like his—a trifle large. For even though she was adopted, she was all the same a Weir. His cousin's child, born out of wedlock. Jeanette's. But she had long ago come to seem really his. His and Enid's.

"There's a new girl in school," said Maggie. "Katrina Howland. She's from New York City. She's not very friendly, I think she's awfully stuck up."

"Howland." Enid frowned. "Yes, someone was telling me —they were from here. A long time ago. And he died."

"Yes. Ted Howland." It was easy, Gil found. "He was a couple of classes ahead of me in school, but we played on the basketball team together. He died about two years ago. Heart attack."

"Katrina says her mother's an old friend of yours," Maggie contributed, looking at her father.

"Yes. I dated her some in high school," he said, feeling as if he were confessing to some major crime, yet knowing that he must tell *some* of the truth because Enid would hear a lot more of it from other quarters.

A forkful of food paused for a moment, halfway to Enid's mouth, but all she said, after she'd chewed and swallowed it, was, "Did you know she was back in town, Gil?"

"Well, yes, as a matter of fact. I ran into her downtown the other day."

"You did?" She laid the fork down. "Why is it you never mentioned it?"

"Slipped my mind, I guess." And he knew that didn't sound right. You don't run into an old girlfriend you haven't seen in twenty-some-odd years and hear that she's moved back to town, and then just totally forget about it. In a town like Selkirk, an old girlfriend was news.

"What's she like?" Enid asked him.

"Like? Oh, I don't know. She was a very nice girl back when I knew her. Looked like she hadn't changed much—a little older like all of us, I guess. We hardly had what I'd call a conversation—not standing on the corner of Main and Pershing waiting for the light to change. She mentioned her little girl—said that's why she's come back. Doesn't feel New York City's any place to bring up a child."

Enid shifted her attention back to Maggie. "Is she—the little Howland girl—overly sophisticated? Coming from the East and the city?"

Maggie considered. "Not that, I think. She just acts like she's better than anybody else. She went to private school in New York. Maybe that's partly what's wrong with her."

Gil laughed. "Maybe she just feels like a fish out of water, here. Don't be so hard on her."

The subject of Cinny Howland's return seemed, after all, to have been safely negotiated, Gil thought with an inner sigh.

He was wrong.

It was the following day that Enid dropped over to Beth Towse's.

On this particular bright, hot morning, when Enid had knocked on the Towse screendoor and, getting no response, opening it and stepped in, calling "*Whoo*-whoo!" the way people do in Selkirk, to find Beth running breathless down the stairs with a dustcloth in her hand but every blond wavelet and curl in place as always, giving somewhat the effect that she was wearing one of the new stretch wigs, but she was not, her hair always looked like that, the subject which at once came up was neither her cad of a husband nor her failed marriage, but an item of local social news.

"No coffee?" she said when Enid had refused her offer of some. "I guess you're right, it is too hot." She settled herself opposite her friend; Enid had taken the sofa, Beth sat in the chair which matched it, fingering the piping and viewing the flowered pattern of the slipcover with distaste, muttering in an aside, "And to think I made these myself. Trying to save his money so he could take that trollop Patty out and wine and dine her. If I'd of known, I'd have gotten them custom made." Her attention shifted to her caller. "I suppose you've heard, haven't you, Enid? That Cinny Neiswanner has come back to Selkirk—to stay?"

"Sinny Ni—" Enid broke off, as light dawned. "Oh, is that who she is? Howland? Mrs. Howland?"

"Yes. Only I still think of her as Cynthia Neiswanner—after all she never lived here after she married Ted Howland. They went East. She's Gil's old flame, you know."

"Yes, I know that. People were careful to tell me, naturally, when I first came here, that I was lucky to get him, because he'd almost married a local girl. Only I didn't remember what her name was now—just what it used to be. Neiswanner . . ."

"And looking not a day older, they tell me," said Beth viciously, with a gleam in her eye. But whether the gleam was the light of battle, to be joined against the enemy, the predatory females of the world, or was instead simply the light of triumph as Beth welcomed someone else into her vale of misery—for misery does love company—Enid did not know.

"Actually she is a little younger than the rest of us . . . seems to me she was only in tenth grade the year Fred and Gil and I were seniors . . ." Beth gazed back, into her vanished youth.

Cinny Neiswanner—a girl who had haunted Enid's early years with Gil; especially after quarrels. And last week he had run into her on the street—and then had *forgotten* he'd seen her? Oh, no. *Slipped my mind, I guess . . .*

And looking not a day older, they tell me . . .

I was telling your son, Mrs. Weir . . .

Chapter 3

It was that same week that Sidney Strait, the new head librarian, again ran afoul of Enid Weir. Over a lost book.

He smiled politely and ran his tongue over his lips as he faced Mrs. Weir and her little girl from behind the desk which had been the gift of Mrs. Weir's mother-in-law. "Now what seems to be the trouble?" he asked pleasantly.

But all the pleasantness in the world wouldn't have solved the problem.

"The *library*," said Mrs. Weir, her face mottled with anger, "has as good as *accused* me of *stealing* a *book!*"

"Oh, now—a routine overdue notice is—"

"I explained a *month* ago that the book had been returned. *The Trees*. Conrad Richter. We don't *have* it, Mr. Strait—"

"Of course not. If you say you returned it, I expect it's simply mislaid."

"Then we'll *look* for it—*won't* we!" And with Sid at her elbow, she searched the library—to his acute embarrassment finding the missing volume in the Young Adult section. With the wrong card in its pocket.

Unfortunately this episode was followed by another, somewhat similar—though the book was not found. (The recovery of *Little Women* weeks later, from behind Maggie's chest of drawers, was too late to be of help to anyone.) It was after this second fracas that Enid undertook a campaign to undermine Sidney Strait; with the best of intentions, and motivated not at all by her dislike of him or by the injury he had done her pride. She simply felt quite honestly that he was incompetent.

He had come to Selkirk from the Maybridge Public Library. So since Gil had a cousin in Maybridge, she began by making inquiries through her; and, at the same time, talking earnestly to one or two members of the Selkirk Library Board.

By October Gil's life had settled into a manageable but horrible pattern. Try to stay out of trouble, was the watchword, the motto, the goal of his days. *Never* tell Enid you've had an attractive female client in your office. Never *never* suggest that you be the one to pick up Maggie from Trina Howland's house—or drop her off—because the girls had by now become fast friends, the truth having turned out to be not that Trina was stuck-up, but that she had thought no one in Selkirk liked her.

In mid-October there was the disastrous P.T.A. meeting which he attended in Enid's place when she was sick in bed with gastrointestinal something; at Maggie's insistence, because her art work was on view in the main exhibit case in the corridor outside the gym.

A cup of coffee in hand, Gil was inspecting the watercolor in question, when Cinny Howland came up beside him.

"School's changed a good deal since our day, hasn't it," she said. She was wearing a green suit, very becoming, which set off her blond hair. She was still almost as slim as she'd been in high-school days, he noted again. Still had good legs.

"Yes. The town outgrew our old junior high some time ago."

"Your wife's not here?"

"No. Ailing with something."

"I'm sorry."

People were streaming into the gym, now, where rows of folding chairs had been set up, and they were gathered into the flooding tide of parents and carried inside. The place was packed, but Gil managed to find seats for them near the back.

Which Enid unfortunately learned all about with no delay.

"You could have *told* me you spent the whole meeting with Cynthia Howland—coffee before, and then sitting with her through the *whole* evening, as big as life, so everyone could look around and say, oh, there's Gil Weir with his old girlfriend, just like old times."

"For Christ's sake, I was standing with her in the hall, we walked into the gym together, and we were barely able to grab about the last two chairs left. Which happened to be together, I didn't think anything about it. Nor did anyone else there, I'm quite sure."

"Oh, yes they did—or I wouldn't have heard about it so fast."

"Stupid gossip—that's all. If not enough happens in this town, people make up something—"

"Like you and Barbara Dresser. That wasn't made—"

"Oh, my God! Not that again! If I'm supposed to be so involved with Barbara, how come I'm all of a sudden so interested in Cynthia Neiswanner? . . . Howland?"

"I was thinking of asking you that myself."

"Oh, my God!" He had stalked out of the room in a fruitless rage, and Enid had gone to bed with a sinus headache.

"Barbara—" Henrietta toyed with the straws of her milkshake. "I don't like to pry . . . but I've been wondering how things are with Gil these days. Are you worried about the competition?"

Barbara took a bite of her sandwich while she thought about an answer to that one. She had never actually *told* Henrietta anything. She had only implied. Because it was better, she had felt, to be suspected of having an affair than to be universally considered an untouchable. A matter of self-respect, really? Yet Enid's campaign of surveillance had upset her. All those telephone calls—Enid forever trying to track Gil down; and her popping into the office, and eyeing Barbara speculatively . . . Barbara had become worried, actually, that Henrietta might have let slip something; and if, consequently, Gil came to hear of his secretary's romantic gabblings to her friend . . . Earlier in the fall, Barbara had even considered backing out of the "affair," with the excuse, to Henrietta, that she hadn't the heart to break up a marriage.

And then Cynthia Howland had ruined that idea. There had been first speculation, then actual rumor. This was not the time to throw in the sponge; Henrietta would think she'd been beaten out by the classy lady from New York.

So Barbara smiled confidently now, at her friend. "The competition?" She touched the knot of hair at the back of her neck. "You mean Cynthia Howland. People are bound to talk, I suppose, just because the two of them were a big thing years ago—but that's *all* it is."

Still, maybe she should just add a few brushstrokes to the picture of herself as a girl who could pick and choose among the men around her. "Of course," she said, "there is Sidney Strait—the new library head? He's single to start with . . ."

"You've met him? Besides just taking out a book, I mean."

"Oh, yes—we're well acquainted." (Hardly true, unfortunately.)

"What's he like?"

"Oh—nice. Shy of girls, I'd say. I get the impression, though, that with a little encouragement . . ."

Actually she had it backward, in this exchange. *She* had been the one who was shy. She had panicked, the day he came into the office to see Gil—panicked, because Sidney Strait was single, and any conversation with a single man might eventually lead somewhere.

"How do you like Selkirk?" she'd asked him.

"Nice town. Though I haven't gotten to know people well just yet. That takes a little time." The blue eyes behind the glasses had rested on her with a little smile, encouraging her to say something friendly. But what?

"Yes, I guess so." Inspired remark. Unable to think of anything else to say, let alone any sparkling repartee, she had resumed her typing while he waited for Gil. Had watched him get up to leave, a little later—a neat, stocky man, not very tall, certainly, but goodness, that didn't matter.

"I can't wait any longer for Mr. Weir. Got to get back to the library. I'll see him some other time."

He had gone. A missed opportunity. Why couldn't she talk to eligible men?

Nor had he come back, either, as he'd said he would.

Henrietta was getting fat. Didn't she know she was?

It was on a day in November that Beth Towse dropped over to the Weirs' for a chat with Enid.

It was a gray day, with most of the leaves gone from the trees, just a few brown ones fluttering here and there on the branches of the oaks, as she parked at the curb and at 4:05 went up the walk to the Weirs' low, mansard-roofed red brick house. There was no answer when she pressed the button of the door chimes, so after three tries she opened the big white door under the fanlight and went in. If Enid were running the vacuum, she wouldn't hear the chimes. Or she could be on the telephone . . .

"*Whoo*—whoo! Enid! It's me." She stood waiting in the tiled entry, cocking an ear for some sound. There was only the ticking of the grandfather's clock (a reproduction) at her elbow.

"Enid?" She stepped forward (it was then 4:08), looking through the archway into the living room, and said, "Oh!" on an intake of breath.

The floor lamp just inside had been knocked over, and lay with its shade askew and the reflector glass broken.

Beth stepped into the room. A chair was shoved out of place, and beside it a table lamp lay smashed. Beyond, sprawled on the textured beige carpeting, lay Enid Weir. No doubt that she was dead; no doubt at all in Beth's mind. Something wrong with her forehead. She'd been shot?

Beth Towse turned and tottered to the phone in the entry. Her hand shook so that she could hardly dial 0 for operator.

"I want the police."

Chapter 4

IT HAD BEEN at about 2:30 that afternoon that Gil, opening the door of his car, which stood in the lot behind his office building, caught sight of Cinny Howland approaching, walking between the rows of parked cars.

"Hi."

"Oh, hello, Gil."

Without his even attempting to analyze why, the November wind seemed to turn bracing instead of chill, the day itself cozy rather than gray. Nor was there any urgency—certainly not—about getting out to see the client who needed a codicil tacked onto her will; he hadn't even told old Mrs. McCutcheon he was coming today.

"How's it seem by now, being back?"

"Oh—different. It's true, I find, that you can't go home again. Home here was twenty years ago: my family, our old house." Mr. Neiswanner had died years before, and Mrs. Neiswanner, after Cinny's marriage, had moved to New York to be near her daughter, and she too was dead now. "Aunt Lucille's been wonderful, but—well, it's her house, not mine. I'm looking for a place of our own, now, for Trina and me. You know the Fenton house?"

"Isn't that kind of far out of town?"

"Not really. The town's spreading that way, you know. But —I'm not sure about it. The house is fine—remodeled several years ago. But I have to take all that land, too. Maybe it's a good investment, and then maybe I'd be foolish to get involved in anything so complicated. Mrs. Fenton decided the place was too much for her, all alone—she's living with her daughter now. But she says I could sell off part of the land . . . Would you take a look at it, Gil? See what you'd advise?"

"Be glad to. Anytime you'd like."

She dangled a key, wired to a crumpled tag, in front of him. "I suppose you're busy right now . . ."

"Nothing I can't do afterward—or another day. Were you going straight out there now?"

"I am if you'll come too."

He considered. "Why don't I meet you? Then I can go on from there and finish up my other business."

"Thanks." She grinned. "See you there, then."

Even going in separate cars he felt a little guilty. As though he'd planned it. Assignation was not a word much employed around Indiana, but it was the one that kept coming to mind on his way out to the Fenton place.

It was a good house, as she'd said. Brick, painted white; an old house, the kind with high-ceilinged rooms, and windows to the floor, and inside shutters, and with wooden lacework over the doors.

"I love it!" Cinny said, gazing about.

"I don't blame you. It's beautiful. I've always admired this house, even when it was the Elders' place—before the brick was painted, and when there was cardboard stuck in the broken windows, and they had a pen in the front yard for the chickens. Remember?"

"I remember. And there were always at least two broken-down cars sitting in the ruts by the porch."

"Mrs. Fenton knows how much it's worth now, I suppose?"

"Oh, she knows! And she's right. It's the extra land that worries me."

They went out and looked at it. Flat and fertile.

"Good land," said Gil.

"Yes, I know. Only I hardly want to farm. I was wondering if I could rent acreage to an adjacent farmer."

They discussed it, and looked everything over. The barn was a wreck and would have to come down. But there was a large shed, newer, in good condition, where farm equipment had once been kept.

"That's the real reason we want this place." Cinny nodded at the shed. "Trina wants a horse."

They leaned against the zigzag rail fence—silvery gray, splintery, dry as the skin of a snake.

"I'm glad you sound so definite about staying on in Selkirk."

"Well, I won't go back to New York. Trina likes it here now. She didn't at first—she wept buckets. We've Maggie to thank for the improvement. She's a darling girl, your Maggie."

He grinned. "We think so!"

"She told me she's adopted."

"Yes."

"I was surprised. She looks like you. But then the adoption agencies do a wonderful job—don't you think?—of matching babies to parents."

He changed the subject. For not even Maggie knew they were related—she and her father. Best for her not to know where she had come from. Born out of wedlock . . .

They had finished looking at the property. Yet he lingered. It was so pleasant, just chatting with Cinny like this. And how easy it was to slip back into the old feeling of closeness. It was with a start that he suddenly remembered he'd been married to someone else for twenty years. And that he shouldn't be here.

"Cinny—" He hesitated. "Can I ask a favor of you?"

"Yes—what?"

"Don't tell anyone I came out here with you."

He could almost see, in her clear, amber eyes, the series of thoughts that went through her head, and then she said, "Oh." She looked down, scuffing a stone back and forth with her loafer. "I guess I'm too used to New York, where no one notices what you do, or cares. Gossip. I should have thought about it." She gave a wry smile. "Is that why we came in separate cars?"

"Actually, no." (Wasn't it? He felt a little sheepish.) "But it's just as well we did."

"Oh, really, Gil! You mean just because we dated each other twenty-some-odd years ago, people think—"

"It was our sitting together at the P.T.A. meeting that started the talk, I gather . . ." He saw that she was laughing.

"I'm sorry, Gil. I just thought, a P.T.A. meeting—well, that's the *last* place I'd think it was possible to get into trouble. But I believe you."

She was leaning back against the rail fence, looking amazingly unchanged from the girl he'd been in love with long ago.

"Cinny—" He spoke on impulse, having had no idea, even a moment ago, that he was going to say this. "You can't imagine how cut up I was when you wrote me you were going to marry Ted."

She smiled—like a small girl who has received an unexpected present. "Were you, Gil? I should feel sorry, but I don't. It's too late to be sorry—you're long since over it. It's just—touching, somehow, at this stage of my life, to be told that someone cared about me that much at one time. I'd hate to think you hadn't even minded!"

But he was looking at her seriously. "Yes, I thought I was over it. If anyone had asked me, during these past years, I'd have said yes. And believed it. But now—"

There was a moment of silence as they faced each other in a suddenly changed situation.

"Oh, Gil—" Distressed, she swung away from him, to stare at the barn, with its sagging roofline, set against the lowering sky.

"Cinny?" He turned her to him, found her lips, felt ferociously happy, fell into despair, kissed her harder, decided that she *must* be not only his past but his future as well, reasoned that Enid had pushed him into it, if she thought he was doing this anyhow (with Barbara? with Barbara *and* Cinny?), he might as well actually, hadn't he? and perceived that his whole life had changed, he was a new man.

She broke away. And the look in her eyes restored him at once to sanity.

"I shouldn't have asked you to come out here." With fingers that trembled she pushed the hair back from her face, which was ashen. "An error in judgment. Tempting fate? Maybe I wanted to, and didn't know it. But this is impossible, Gil. It's dangerous. You see, you don't know what it's been like for me, being widowed. It's so lonely. Terribly lonely. I've adjusted to it, to some extent. But *this—you* . . . you've disrupted everything. Don't you see?"

"Then we'll go on from here. I didn't mean this to happen —honestly, Cinny. It just did—"

She smiled rather cynically through the tears that stood in her eyes and said, "Don't tell me it's bigger than both of us! Not one of those nifty rationalizations. Let's be adult, shall we? Instead of acting like a couple of love-struck high-school kids."

A recollection of the goofy, dazzled look Fred Towse had worn flicked through Gil's mind, and was gone; this was not the same thing at all. "Look, Cinny. My marriage has been falling apart since—since I don't know how long; certainly since sometime this summer. Nothing to do with you. Enid's —I get to thinking some of the time that she's out of her mind. She makes these crazy accusations. She checks up on me—constantly. She convinced herself somehow that I was having an affair with my secretary—"

"And were you?" She seemed half-serious, half-amused.

"For God's sake, no! I've never even looked at another woman since I married Enid."

"Um." The gesture she made with her hand ended palm

up, fingers spread, indicating the two of them. "So how did *this* happen?"

He caught her hand; held it. "I didn't finish. Till I saw *you*. On Main Street, waiting for the light to change. I never even *noticed* another woman till—"

She looked at him a moment, almost malevolently, then snatched her hand away. "It's only making things worse, standing here talking about it. I ought to know better! Blowing up a small incident into a Very Big Thing. I don't want to hear any more, Gil. And by tomorrow you'll be glad I didn't."

She turned and started toward her car. He caught up with her, took her by the arm. "Cinny! You can't walk out on me now! I can't—can't do without you. I swear!"

She shook him off. "I'm not a homewrecker, Gil. You say any more, and I'll have to go back to New York—whether I like it or not." She stopped as she reached her car, and looked despairingly at the white-painted house with its long windows. "I guess I'm not buying it—"

"Listen, Cinny—"

"Or if I do, I'll shut myself in and never come out again." She opened her car door and got in. But before driving off she looked him in the eyes kind of ruefully and said, "Thanks, Gil, for coming out. Take it easy." And then she was gone, having, with her last words, reduced the whole episode to just that—an episode. One that was closed now.

Gil got into his car and sat there. What had happened, really? Had he read into Cinny's words, into her reactions, indeed into her physical response when he had kissed her, more than was there? Was it simply a case of a lonely widow momentarily warming to the unexpected presence in her private, rather empty world, of someone she used to know? He knew how it had been from his end, certainly.

But it was hopeless. Even as he thought of the feel of her lips against his, he knew the same thing wouldn't happen again. One move in her direction, and she'd leave town. She'd said so. And Cynthia Neiswanner had always been a girl who meant what she said. You could count on her that way.

He sat on in his car, parked back of the tractor shed in which Trina Howland wanted to keep a horse. Traffic went by on the road, which was a numbered highway—Indiana State Highway 47—but he was oblivious of its passing. Nor did any driver of any car or truck which went by the Fenton house see that anyone was parked there that afternoon. There was the house—to be seen from the road—and the long, low shed with its stout coat of white paint; back of the shed—extending clear to the barn—the rail fence, its rickrack outline surrounding what had once been the pigpen; and the barn itself, leaning tiredly to one side as though the years, and perhaps the weather with them, had been too much. But no one saw a parked car.

"I'm sorry," said Barbara into the telephone, "he's not in."

"This is Lieutenant Hogg"—only he pronounced it Hoag, very carefully—"of the Police Department. Can you tell me where—"

"I'm expecting him back any moment. But he might still be at McCutcheons'—that's the McCutcheon farm, out south of town."

"About how long ago did he leave to go out there?"

"Oh, two hours, I'd say. Would you like me—"

"Never mind. But if he comes in, have him call me." He gave her the number, and with a start she realized it was Gil's home phone.

"*Lieutenant—*"   **1722974**

But he had rung off.

What in the world . . . ? she wondered, making mistake after mistake in her typing because she wasn't paying attention. Had someone broken into the house and stolen Enid's mink coat? Or what?

And then a uniformed officer came in. Bud Ertz. She knew Bud because his family were long-time neighbors of the

Dressers.

"Hi, Barbara. Your boss hasn't showed up yet?"

"No. Listen, what is all this?"

"Mrs. Weir's been shot. Killed."

"You mean *Enid?*"

"Yeah. That's her name, isn't it—Enid. Her."

"Oh, my goodness!" The news went to her head like alcohol. She could hardly restrain that little smile that sometimes overtakes one at such moments—when hearing unexpectedly of a tragedy not one's own. The pure excitement of it, and the prospect of being the first to pass it on to someone else—

"What *happened?* Do they know *who*—"

"No, they don't know who."

"Oh, dear! Poor Gil! I wonder if they reached him at Mrs. McCutcheon's—"

"No, they didn't. He hadn't gone there—at least he hasn't yet."

"But he said—" Barbara stopped in midsentence. She *couldn't* be mistaken about what he'd said, because she'd gotten the will out for him, and he'd glanced at it and stuck it in his briefcase.

So why hadn't he gone there? Where had he been for the past two hours? No—more than two hours. A possible answer occurred to her and she shoved it away as not possible, but a sudden chill had come over her and she put a hand to her forehead and leaned over her desk, feeling a little sick.

By the time Gil got out to the McCutcheon place the overcast day was already thickening into dusk. The door of the big white barn was closed, the barnyard deserted, and although a dim light glimmered through one window toward the rear of the house, Gil at first wondered whether anyone was at home. Three geese followed him to the front door, and stood there honking at him, one looking as if it might nip him with its great, solid-looking yellow bill. He said, "Shoo!"

and made a threatening movement with his hand, but the trio only stood fast, sticking their necks out ever farther.

At last he heard the creaking of flood boards inside, and a face appeared at the murky square of glass. The door opened.

"Oh, it's you, Gilman." Mrs. McCutcheon had known him all his life; for years his mother had bought fresh chickens from her.

"Come in, won't you? I thought you might be coming. Now why was that?" She stood stock-still, thinking. "You didn't call me on the telephone, did you?" She clicked on a pair of light brackets graced by old, discolored parchment shades, and the small, square living room, with its flowered wallpaper, emerged reluctantly into shabby life.

"No, I didn't call. My secretary may have, I don't know."

"No, she didn't. It was a man called. *That's* it. Now I remember. Wanted to know if you was here, and I thought he must have the wrong number, or else dialed here by mistake."

"Did he say who it was? My secretary must have told someone I could perhaps be reached here."

"Yes, I thought something like that might be the case. After I hung up, I decided you must be expected out here, prob'ly. That's why it come as no surprise when I seen you at the door."

She was sitting in an old rocker, now, rocking. She was dressed the way farm women used to dress when he was a boy, not the way they did nowadays, as smart as anyone else. A long cotton print in blue and white, in a small design of spriggy flowers, tied at the waist with a stringy belt of the same; and on her feet, shapeless old black, laced-up oxfords, with fat bulging out over their tops.

"Who was it who called me, Mrs. McCutcheon?" Gil tried again.

"Who—? Oh, let's see, now. Funny name, seems t'me. I never heard it before. Nobody *I* know. Now, let me see—Mr. Tenahoe? *Louie* Tenahoe, I think. Or Tenahode? Something

37

like that—"

Gil smiled patiently. "Well, never mind, Mrs. McCutcheon —I'm sure he'll catch up with me eventually. Now, this codicil . . ."

It did not take long. He promised to draw up what she wanted at once and bring it out for her signature. (No question of her coming into town; her grandson had disqualified her as a passenger—too dangerous, what with cries of "Look out! Oh, Sonny, you'll kill us!" and grabbing his arm.)

He bade old Mrs. McCutcheon good-by, made his way with gingerly caution, among the geese, to his car, accompanied all the way by the sound of honking, got in, and gave his escort a long and vibrating raspberry just before he closed the door —which did not disconcert them in any way, perhaps even giving rise to some idea in their tiny heads that he might be a relative.

He had driven halfway down the lane to the highway when a police car, its rooflight flashing, turned into the opposite end.

Gil backed up, to allow the car entry; cranked down his window, and leaned out, as the State Trooper sprang from his vehicle.

"What's the trouble, officer?"

"Are you Gilman Weir?" the other countered.

"Yes. Yes, I am. What—"

"The Selkirk police contacted us, asked us to locate you. I'm sorry, Mr. Weir: your wife's been shot."

"My *wife!* . . . *Shot?*"

"She's dead, Mr. Weir."

Gil stared at the officer. "She . . . she *can't* be . . ."

"I'm sorry."

His mind was a mosaic of tiny, broken pieces—fragments from his life—on the drive in. The drive home. Home, where Lieutenant Hogg was waiting to ask him some questions.

It wasn't Maggie who had found her; Maggie would have

been at Girl Scouts all afternoon—that he knew. Mrs. Towse—the officer said—had found her. And Gil visualized again the scene Beth Towse would have come upon.

At least the telephone call Mrs. McCutcheon had received was clear now. Not Mr. Louis Tenahoe or Tenahode, but Lieutenant Hogg. Orin Hogg, known as "O.H.," with whom he'd gone to school.

Enid flashed before him—not Enid as she had looked this morning, or this noon at lunch, not Enid lying dead from a bullet wound on the beige carpet of the living room. What he saw was the girl he had met years ago at Columbia, when he'd been a law student and she had been taking her masters at Teachers College. She'd had flyaway light-brown hair, the bloom of youth . . .

Cinny kept coming into his mind, too. Cinny in his arms this afternoon, kissing him back. Cinny walking away from him. *Say any more and I'll go back to New York.*

Guilt. Guilt stifling him, almost; he couldn't shake it off.

A uniformed policeman let him into his own house. There were more cops inside, including redheaded Lieutenant Hogg standing in the middle of the living room, which was a shambles.

Gil nodded. " 'Lo, O.H." Enid wasn't there; they had taken her away. He was relieved yet somehow disapproving—and again, guilty? He had been steeling himself for the ordeal of seeing her there on the floor dead, and for some reason he felt it was something he was supposed to have gone through. Some kind of atonement of which he was now deprived.

"Hello, Gil," said Orin. "Sorry about this. Awfully sorry."

He nodded.

"They've taken her down to—you want to see her later?"

"Yeah. Yeah, thanks." Gratefully he clutched at his hair shirt. He'd go and look at her downtown.

Orin pointed to an area of the floor. "She was there."

Gil stared at the spot indicated as though waiting for it to tell him something, and then they both walked through the vestibule into the dining room, where Orin had evidently been working—a pen and some papers lay on the high-gloss mahogany surface of the dining table. They each pulled out a chair and sat down. It was cheerless indeed, sitting there sharing the unset table with four stiff, empty chairs under the bright light of the chandelier, which was designed to look like burning candles, except that candle flames were never that color nor of such a hard brightness.

"Where's my child?" Gil asked. "I hope she didn't—"

"Oh, no, she hasn't been here. Beth Towse volunteered to see to Maggie—said she'd pick her up from Girl Scouts and take her over to your sister-in-law's."

"Oh, that's good. Fine. That's fine. O.H., do you know who could have—" He gestured toward the living room, and shuddered.

"Not yet. Do you? Any idea?"

"None. No, I can't imagine. Someone breaking in—"

"No one broke in. We're sure of that."

"Walked in, then? We never lock the doors when any of us are home. Only when we're out—and not always then, either."

"You have a gun?"

"Yes, a revolver."

"Where do you keep it?"

"At the back of my sock drawer."

"Mind seeing if it's there?"

"Not at all." He got up and went back into the vestibule and along the hall to the bedrooms. An odd feeling, going into the master bedroom that he would not be sharing anymore with Enid. A sick, clammy, empty feeling, overlaid with disbelief. Enid couldn't be dead; after twenty years with her it wasn't possible.

As he crossed the room he had a fleeting vision of Cinny Howland lying on the quilted coverlet of his bed in a flimsy nightgown.

Oh, dear, no! He mustn't! Though at least she'd had a nightgown on, hadn't she. He hoped that wasn't quite as bad as if she'd had *nothing* on? And he opened the second drawer of the bureau and thrust a hand back behind the socks.

"Not there?" Orin spoke from behind him, in the doorway. And as Gil pulled the drawer out farther and shoved the socks to one side, he wondered whether his friend the lieutenant hadn't already searched these drawers and knew it wasn't there.

"No," he said in a tight voice. "It doesn't seem to be here."

"That's where you always keep it?"

"Yes."

"When did you last see it—as well as you can remember?"

"I haven't seen it in a long time; it's too far back in the drawer. I've felt it when I was looking for a particular pair of socks. When? I don't remember. I never think about the damn thing, actually." He was hunting through all the other drawers, now—not only his, but Enid's.

Of course it wasn't there.

They went back to the dining room.

"Your wife knew where you kept it . . ." A statement, not a question.

"Certainly. Though she'd have no occasion to remove it. No reason she'd have touched it."

"Well, we don't know that. Who else might have known you had a gun?"

"Any friend of mine, I suppose. You know how you get into a casual conversation about something like that. After Kennedy was shot, and there was so much fuss about gun legislation—I'm sure I must have said to one or two people, anyway, 'Sure, I've got a revolver in the house, probably shouldn't have.' Enid, too, might have mentioned it to almost anyone—her sister; I don't know."

"Do you have a permit for it, by the way?"

"Yes. Of course I have."

"Good. Then we've got a record of the serial number."

"You didn't find the gun, I take it. I mean the one she was —was killed with."

"No." Orin Hogg looked down at the notes he had made. "Gil, you're a lawyer, I don't have to warn you that you have the right to remain silent, and anything you say may be held against you, et cetera—only, for the record, consider it said. But Gil, where *were* you this afternoon? You weren't where you told your secretary you'd be."

Gil's mouth quirked up at one corner. "Oh, I was eventually."

O.H.'s eyes narrowed. "You didn't get to the McCutcheon farm till *long* after your wife was dead. Where'd you go when you first left your office?"

"Out to have a look at the Fenton house for a client of mine who's thinking of buying it."

"What time was that?"

"Oh, I left the office around two-thirty. Got out there about a quarter of three, I suppose."

"You went straight there from your office."

"Yes."

"Why didn't you tell Barbara that was where you were going?"

"Because I changed my itinerary. As I was getting into my car, Cynthia Howland happened by and asked me if I'd look at the Fenton property for her and give her some advice. She likes the house but is worried about buying all that land with it."

Gil was sure there'd been a flicker of something in Orin Hogg's face at the mention of Cinny. O.H. was one person who would clearly, very clearly remember the era when he had dated her; he and O.H. had graduated from Selkirk High School in the same class.

"She go out with you to the house?" his old classmate inquired.

He'd decided about that. Definitely. "No," he said. "I

drove out alone to have a look around."

"Mrs. Fenton can bear that out? You got the key from her?"

"No. I haven't talked to Mrs. Fenton about it at all, as yet. And I didn't need a key. As I say, Cynthia's quite satisfied with the house, she didn't ask for my opinion on it, so there was no need to go in. I only looked at the land and the outbuildings. The barn will have to come down, but there's a tractor shed that's fine."

"How long were you there, then, at the Fenton place?"

"Until I left to drive to the McCutcheon farm. That's a fair distance."

"I telephoned Mrs. McCutcheon at four thirty-five and you hadn't yet gotten there."

"I arrived soon after that, I suppose. Must have left the Fenton farm about four-ten, four-fifteen."

"You were at the Fenton place, then, for an hour and a half?"

"I suppose I must have been."

"Doing what? All that time?"

Gil frowned. "Well, I walked around a good bit, looking. Then when I'd finished, I sat in my car for a while working on the summation for a difficult case I've got coming into court next week. Some points occurred to me while I was walking." It was the best he could manage, he'd decided. The summation, in longhand, *was* in his briefcase, and who could prove he hadn't written it this afternoon?

"You mean you were just sitting there in your car, writing?"

Gil shrugged, a little sadly. "I hope it isn't going to be necessary to prove I was?"

"No one saw you there? Do you remember meeting any-one on the road, coming or going?"

Gil leaned forward, his head bent over arms crossed on the table before him. "I'm afraid I didn't notice, O.H."

The police left, at last—after Orin had had someone search

Gil's car for the revolver, but naturally it wasn't there.

Finally Gil was able to close the door on the lot of them, and he at once picked up the phone and called Cinny.

"Oh, Gil, I'm so sorry!" He drew a little comfort from the warmth of her voice. "I've heard, of course. Someone telephoned just now, about Enid. How terrible for you. How's Maggie?"

"I don't know. All right, I think, she's at her aunt's. I'm going over there in a little while. Cinny, I called because I wanted you to be clear about something. You didn't go out to Fentons' with me, I went alone. I saw you in the parking lot downtown, and we discussed the property, and I went out by myself to look at the land for you. I didn't go in the house, I didn't have a key. That's what I've told the police. O.K.?"

There was a short silence. Then, "O.K. I suppose that's best. Gil, do you know yet who—"

"No, they don't know who killed her. Not yet."

"Gil . . . there's no question, is there, of your needing to explain fully where you were? I mean, prove . . . because I was *with* you—"

"No," he said hoarsely. "No, thanks, Cinny, I'll be all right. You stay out of it. I had to mention your name—had to, to be able to say I'd been somewhere, and why. But you won't come into it."

"If there's anything I can do—"

"Thanks, but better not."

"I mean Maggie."

"Yes, O.K. Maggie. Bye, Cin."

Hanging up left him peculiarly, all at once, on his own. As though he'd said an irrevocable good-by to the social world he knew, the friends he'd had. Murder. A conviction for murder waited for someone. Was it for him? The murder of Enid Kinsey Weir.

"And Maggie will stay with us, of course," said Phyll. "You too, Gil?" But she frowned, and he knew she was relieved when he declined.

"I'll be fine at the house. Thanks anyway, Phyll." From the frown, and the darting way in which she kept watching him, he deduced that for herself she was convinced he'd shot and killed her sister. She'd expressed her sympathy, certainly, but guardedly, as though withholding most of it until she found out whether it was by any chance deserved.

"Have just a bit of something, Maggie?" Phyll was leaning down beside her niece with a now-let's-do-this smile, talking to her as though Maggie had suddenly become retarded. "Why not eat something and then you can go up and go to bed. Or go and watch television?"

To everything, Maggie shook her head.

They sat in the kitchen; all meals served at the Strothers' were eaten in the kitchen, or at least since Beejay's departure they had been. Joyce and Bobby, finished with supper, were watching television in the family room, but Maggie, pale-faced and red-eyed, still sat at the table next to her father. Benson, Phyll's oldest boy, was on his second piece of pie.

"Frozen, or from the bakery?" he asked, summing up his own lifetime experience of his mother's culinary proclivities.

"I made it," she said stonily.

Benson was a tall, spindly youth who stooped badly and wore glasses. He should have been a good student, looking, as he did, as though he must have been born slumped over a book; but he was lazy. Now that he was out of high school, though, and unable to go to college, he had apparently developed a great zeal to learn. His mother had been heard to remark that his current preoccupation with ivied halls might not be unconnected with the distaste he had expressed for his job at the Shell station. "A little hard work'll never hurt you," she said periodically. "You'll appreciate your education all the more when you finally make it to college. Maybe you'll even study. And you'll get there; eventually. Just like Marilyn."

"Uncle Gil," Benson began now, "how long will it take

them to settle the estate? I was wondering." Quite pointedly he ignored his mother's warning frown.

"What?" Gil was afraid he hadn't even heard the question. He was going over again how he'd searched all the bedroom drawers with Orin Hogg watching him.

"Aunt Enid's estate. How long will it take to settle it?"

"Benson!" his mother hissed.

"Mom said I shouldn't ask, but—"

"Benson." Phyllis's voice was shrill. "It's extremely thoughtless of you to ask that of your Uncle Gil when—well, this just isn't the time!"

Benson made almost a habit, Gil had noticed, of saying the tactless thing, committing the inopportune act, deliberately irritating his mother or anyone else around. He seemed actually to court disapproval. Sometimes Gil wondered whether this were not a direct result of his having been deserted by his father—a feeling of, look, you'll notice me one way or the other even if he didn't.

"You hoped if you had the tuition money—" Gil began.

"Well, yes." Benson shoveled in the last of his pie. "I could start midterm at I.U. if I had some money. And I could maybe even buy myself a real car to get there in, instead of that junkheap—"

"Benson." His mother's near-black eyes cut through him like laser beams. "You may leave the kitchen. And take Maggie into the family room—she can watch television."

"I'm sorry," she said to Gil when the two of them were left alone. Though he had the feeling she was not sorry on his account, merely disapproving of her son's crassness. "Sometimes I don't know what to do with him. You'd think it was *my* fault his father left us to starve, the way he acts. And he's so bitter because Marilyn's at I.U. instead of him. But I can't afford to send two of them to college at once, not yet. And Joyce and Bobby still to educate, after—"

"But the money you'll be getting from your mother's estate will make a big difference now, won't it?"

There was a moment's pause, and then her answer shocked him with the enmity which underscored the words. "I suppose that's what you've told the police?"

Phyll was afraid . . . ? The distrust he'd sensed earlier, the suspicion, the watchfulness in her darting, covert glances, assumed another possible meaning. He'd thought she was physically apprehensive, believing he could be her sister's killer. But perhaps not—the thing that worried her could be her own position in the puzzle now facing the police: she stood to profit largely by Enid's death. And she saw Gil not as an ally, someone linked to her by family ties, but as an opponent. Phyll Strothers fought her battles alone, and trusted no one—least of all, apparently, her late sister's husband. Only Enid, alive, had linked them together.

"I've told the police nothing about the money. But how they find out makes no difference—your mother's will is a matter of record."

"I did wonder, of course"—she was staring at him coldly; a tigress with young to provide for—"whether you might be planning to sue in court for part of it. Since Maggie was born after—"

"No. Your mother's will was quite clear. You got your half of the estate with no strings attached—"

"Which Beejay spent—all of it . . ."

"And Enid's half, if she died without issue, was to pass to you also—or to your heirs."

"And Maggie doesn't count as issue."

"She does not." Gil sighed, and got up from the table. "It'll all be yours, Phyllis, and you're welcome to it."

There was a light smile on his sister-in-law's mouth, and something else in her eyes—a sort of spiteful look of triumph. Was she thinking of the money? or of the pleasure she felt in depriving him of any further use of it?

"I'd better be going," he said. "And thanks."

He said good night to his daughter, drove home, and reluctantly went into his own house and closed and locked the door—an action which seemed at once futile and symbolic. Locking the door against whom, or what?

He made his way to the master bedroom. No vision of Cinny on the bed. Nor of Enid as she had looked when he'd stopped in at the morgue before going over to Phyll Strothers'.

And he thought of Lieutenant Orin Hogg, working late over this murder case, no doubt, downtown at the City Building.

Chapter 5

IN HER BEDROOM on the second floor of the French-style mansion Joel Davis, Senior, had built in Indianapolis some forty-five years before, to dramatize his rise in the business world, Jeanette Weir Davis, who was married to Joel Davis, Junior—now the only Davis left since the death of his father —stood at the tall, expensively draped windows looking at the Indianapolis *Star,* which the maid had brought up with her morning juice and coffee.

The juice and coffee were untouched on their silver tray. Jeanette couldn't have swallowed a thing. She read the account of the murder over again, carefully, and then stared for quite some time at the picture of Enid Weir. The woman who had been all these years in possession of her daughter— her own daughter Margaret.

She'd never dreamed, certainly, that she'd be unable to have another baby. And doctor after doctor, in recent years, had said there was no apparent reason. "No reason, Mrs. Davis, that you can't have a baby. It may be your husband, you know. If he were tested—"

"Oh, no." Hastily. "No, he wouldn't want that, I'm sure." She wouldn't dare ever to suggest to Joel that he might not be able—

Margaret. Little Margaret. Not so little now: twelve.

She should have gotten up the nerve to tell Joel long ago. Wasn't eleven years long enough to be sure of him? And besides, his ogre of a father who'd been such a stickler for everything being flawless, picky-proper, and solid gold, was dead now. And she was remembering with all the familiar, long-concealed dislike, the old man, stronger than ever the older he'd gotten, handsome like his son, but white-haired, with wild eyebrows like horns growing from his forehead . . . Yes, what was she afraid of, with Joel, Senior, gone?

If she had told Joel earlier . . . But every time she'd tried to frame the explanation it sounded worse to her. She had braced herself to tell him; even opened her mouth to begin. But then the impulse had frozen in her throat, and died, and she'd ended up, in a rush of relief, saying something else entirely.

She had wondered, often, how it could work out—ever. But today for the first time everything seemed clear and simple. Jeanette had known, always, that Enid Weir would fight like a madwoman to keep the child that wasn't even hers; but now she was dead, an obstacle no longer, and Jeannette couldn't feel even the least regret on that score. All that remained to be done was to break the news to Joel. Surely, surely, it would be all right with him? In any case she had already made the decision; or the decision had made itself, and was taking her with it?

Her heart bled not a drop for her own flesh and blood left grieving and miserable over the loss of the only mother the child had ever known; perhaps because she, Jeanette Davis, was already visualizing joyous scenes of reunion, child-ish wounds all bound up and magically cured, the millennium for everyone—*You mean you're my real mother and I'm to come and live with you?* Oh, happy, happy!

Because by one means and another, Jeanette Weir had always managed to get, eventually, everything she wanted.

Barbara had come early to the office this morning. By daylight the fact of murder so close at hand did not seem quite so unnerving. And tragedy—someone else's—can be highly stimulating, lifting one, for a change, quite out of the humdrum. She worked on through the morning in almost a glow.

Occasionally that little question—the cold, ugly, slimy one —crawled through the bottom of her thoughts: had he killed his wife? could he have? But she resolutely refused to recognize it, tried even to deny that she'd had such a doubt—it would have been unworthy of her. Once when she wasn't quite quick enough to avoid the question when it came by again, she even answered it—to prove to herself that she couldn't possibly have any doubts: of course he hadn't, because if the police thought he had they'd have arrested him. Wouldn't they?

Interesting, thought Orin Hogg as he watched his informant, leaving his office, go on through the Headquarters lobby past the officer on duty at the communications desk, and out into the corridor of the City Building. Ernestine Fitchly—who had come in voluntarily with her information.

O.H. had heard gossip, at least speculation, concerning Gil and Cynthia Neiswanner—Cynthia Howland—since her return to Selkirk; but he had put that down to idle chatter, stemming purely from the female tendency to make a romance of everything. But Barbara Dresser. The first he'd heard of anything there. And Henrietta Fitchly should know, shouldn't she? She was Barbara's best friend . . .

You could never be sure, could you, of what people might be doing on the side—like Fred Towse, who had certainly surprised everyone. Had Gil Weir been leading a double life, and no one the wiser? Or almost no one . . .

Gil sat with Orin Hogg in his office at Police Headquarters. There seemed to be no real leads, Orin said, in the case as yet . . .

"It seems to be common knowledge around town, Gil, that your wife had money of her own."

"Yes, she did have."

"You inherit, of course?"

"I don't get a penny of it." Gil frowned quizzically. "That surprised you, didn't it." He explained about his late mother-in-law's will, with Enid's half of the estate held in trust, so that she'd had only the income from it. "And since Enid died without issue—Maggie isn't ours, you know—her share goes to her sister. To Phyllis."

"I see. How much money is involved?"

"It's invested, all of it; value at present is probably in the neighborhood of a hundred and sixty thousand."

O.H. whistled. "Quite a chunk. Does that go outright to Mrs. Strothers or again only the income?"

"Outright. The only reason for leaving it tied up in the first place was Mrs. Kinsey's desire to pass on her money exclusively to her own family; not to me, for instance. Phyllis had three children, Enid had none, at the time of their mother's death. Mrs. Kinsey was convinced, when she had the will drawn up, that Enid would not produce any children. Hence the provisions—"

"Um. Yes. You're not contesting on Maggie's account? Since the intent was to provide for the grandchildren—how do the courts see adoptive children in a case like that?"

"Issue is a clear legal term, meaning lineal descendant; in a will it is a word of limitation, equivalent to 'heirs of the body.' Anyhow, Mrs. Kinsey's intent was clear from the wording of the will: it was to provide for her own flesh and blood, no one else's." He shrugged. "The Strothers kids need the money anyway. Maggie and I don't." Nor did he add the fact that made the full truth slightly different, even, from what Orin Hogg supposed it to be: that legally Maggie wasn't even his. Jeanette had refused to sign adoption papers.

"Of course she's yours to keep," Jeanette had said. "Do you think I'd ever want my so-called 'past' messing up my future? But as to signing my name on a piece of paper—like making out a bill of sale for *my* baby with my eyes and my coloring, and my blood in her—no, I can't do that. You'll just have to take my word for it that I won't ever want her back."

And Enid—oh, there was no other baby for Enid; she'd counted on this one all through Jeanette's pregnancy. The fact that Maggie was actually a Weir . . . So they had taken Maggie on Jeanette's terms.

"You and your wife were getting on all right were you, Gil?" O.H. inquired. "No domestic troubles?"

"No troubles—no." And he wondered whether Orin would find out differently. Had Enid aired her grievances, real or fancied, outside her own home? He had no way of knowing; and it would be stupid to set O.H. onto a scent if the trail hadn't even been laid; he'd wait, and see whether he picked it up for himself.

The lieutenant's phone rang. And with quickening interest Gil listened to Orin's end of the ensuing conversation.

O.H. hung up. "We may be in luck. A man who was arrested for car theft, in Chicago, claims he shot and killed your wife."

"Ah. Does it seem likely?"

The other shrugged. "You know about confessions. Maybe he killed her, maybe he didn't. They're checking out the details."

"What's the man's name?"

"Lemseider." Orin glanced for corroboration at the name he had jotted down. "Clark Lemseider."

Gil searched his memory. "Never heard of him . . ."

"He's got one fact right. Claims he fired twice. There was a second bullet, besides the one that struck your wife; we dug it out of the plaster near the bay window. I didn't give out that particular piece of information to the news media, so this fellow can't have learned it from the papers. He doesn't have the gun, of course; says he threw it in the lake. Lake Michigan."

"Did he say why he—"

"Says he was looking for money, or jewelry, furs—anything like that—and she surprised him. Could be. You told me you found nothing missing from the house?"

"Nothing—as far as I've noticed. Except the revolver."

"Which was a Smith and Wesson thirty-two."

"Yes."

"Same caliber as the weapon your wife was killed with."

"Oh—you know that for sure now?"

"Yes. There's the slug from the plaster in your living room, and the doctor sent over the other one, from the autopsy, a little while ago." He looked up, studying Gil from under his auburn eyebrows. "Well, we'll see—about this man Lemseider."

Maybe, thought Gil, just maybe, a lucky break.

In a jail cell in Chicago, some hundred and sixty miles away, sat a fifty-five-year-old man—clean-shaven, with thinning hair and with poppy eyes set too far apart. He was smiling. He always smiled—it was an expression that never left his face—but just now he was smiling a little more than usual.

They'd be back for him soon, he guessed. There'd be another interrogation session. He imagined he'd got 'em going in circles.

"You don't believe me?" he'd said. "You'd better. Because I done it, I tell you. I killed that woman in Selkirk. Just ask me about it. Ask me—I'll tell you."

Thought they were going to sentence him again for car theft, did they? Story of his life—always getting into trouble for some piddling little thing. Never anything of consequence, something that'd make 'em sit up and take notice. When they knew what you were in for, in the pen, they treated you like you was nothing. Car stealing—kid stuff, that was all.

Well, this time he was going to get a little respect. Let 'em sit up and take notice. If he was going inside—and he didn't think there was much doubt about *that*—it'd be for something big. Murder.

He felt more important just thinking about it. A little more thinking, and he'd even believe it himself, that he'd killed a woman—that Mrs. Weir.

She had dressed with special care, in a full, long skirt and demure white blouse with ruffles at wrist and neck. Her dark hair was swept up in an Empress Josephine style, with tendrils escaping artfully in front of the ears and at the neck, giving her an old-fashioned look which seemed just right for the occasion.

As she came down the circular stairway late in the afternoon, she rested a hand lightly on the polished stair rail, feeling almost lovingly the smooth wood beneath her fingers. Surely all this—this house, this wealth, Joel—would not be taken from her? Not after all this time . . . Why, she held him in the palm of her hand; always had.

He'd called her this morning, from his office. "Have you seen today's paper?"

"Yes. Joel—"

"Isn't that woman who was murdered in Selkirk a cousin of yours? Her husband, I mean. Isn't he a cousin?"

"Yes. Gil Weir." So he already knew. About Enid's death.

"I'm sorry. Or didn't you know her well?"

"I'd met her a couple of times, that's all. But—a terrible thing, isn't it, her being murdered like that . . . and in all the papers." She'd told him she'd send flowers . . .

This evening when Joel came home, she'd break the news, at last, about Margaret. She'd gamble *everything*. Everything.

She went into the elegant white living room, where Ruby, the maid, had turned on the lamps at first dusk. Everywhere in the room, white on white—white satin brocade, white velvet, deep-pile white carpeting. The perfect background chosen by the decorator to set off Jeanette's vivid beauty. Everything Scotch-garded, of course. (Except me? she thought darkly.)

He was late.

Finally he came, and by then her hands were icy cold.

He was a rather fleshy young man, handsome to the point of redundancy, an effect not so much of feature as of quantity: going on the theory that you can't have too much of a good thing, Nature had made more of him. And he was not all that young, as a matter of fact, having by now passed forty, but the impression he gave was that of a slightly beefy twenty-six-year-old. Perhaps the lush ripeness of his face precluded the formation of wrinkles.

He kissed her, and was clearly gratified at the ardent response.

"Cold hands, warm heart?" he queried her. "What's the matter?"

"Nothing's the matter," she said, drawing back and looking up at him while she kept a hand on his sleeve. "Everything's very right, if you'll see it that way too. You *must!* You *must,* Joel!"

"*What* must I?"

"Well, first, you've got to remember that I love you. You know that, don't you? There's never been a moment since I met you that you haven't been the most important thing in the world to me."

He was frowning, a look which made him almost handsomer, like some perplexed god. "What are you getting at, dear? You've bought something, like a race horse? Or you've decided to have a career?"

"Oh, no, Joel. This is serious."

"You smashed up the Mercedes."

"No. Sit down." She seated herself in a small brocade-upholstered chair, and Joel sank onto the soft white cushions of the sofa.

"Have *I* done something?" he asked grimly.

She shook her head, and told him. About being engaged to someone else, before she'd met him. About breaking up with the boy. "No one—I've told you, Joel, and it's true—no one, before you, was the right man for me." The pregnancy discovered then, and she had refused to tell her discarded lover, refused to patch things up.

"So I had the baby. No one here knew—no one but my own family. Mother told people I'd gone to Minneapolis to take care of my grandmother, and that I was going to business college there. All of which was true—I did take a business course; only, I needed my grandmother more than she needed me."

She could see how upset Joel was. He watched her fixedly, kneading his hands together, and his fingers were trembling.

"What did you do with the baby?"

"I gave her to my cousin Gil and his wife. The Enid Weir who was killed yesterday . . ." She faltered and stopped. Searched his face for some clue to the future. Would he turn from her—alienated, implacable? Would he turn on her—angry, hurt beyond hope of repair? He was so touchy—oh, she knew that, she had used the fact to bind him to her, had built him up when his father had torn him down, time and again. If he felt now that she had betrayed him . . .

"My little girl's name is Margaret." He voice was almost a whisper. "She's twelve years old, Joel, and—oh, darling, when I saw the news in the paper this morning I knew the time had come! She's ours—mine and yours, the child we've always wanted! Do you see? She has no foster mother, now that Enid's dead; we can take her back."

He had put his hand over his eyes, as though shielding them from some harsh light. "Why didn't you ever tell me?"

"*Tell* you? Darling, how could I? Telling you before we were married would have stopped the wedding. Permanently. The high and mighty Davis family, accepting an unwed mother? Oh, no. And after we were married—well, we expected to have our own babies, didn't we. But we haven't—my fault, maybe; it could be something went wrong when I had Margaret. So now—I want her back. Joel . . . Joel, tell me you understand; that I haven't done anything too —awful to you?"

He looked up then, through a glitter of unacknowledged tears, and she felt a surge of almost giddy relief. She had gambled and she had not lost. No, *he* had lost: she had wounded him grievously. She was moved—not by compassion, not by contrition, but by awe at her own power to inflict injury. The naked misery she saw in the soft brown eyes of her husband gave her an instant feeling of triumph, of warmth, of safety.

Just as always, she held him in the palm of her hand. The only difference was that she knew now that he would not escape. (Had he always known that?)

She went on her knees beside him. "Say it's all right, Joel?"

He took her in his arms, his cheek against her hair. "You could have told me—long ago. It would've been all right."

"I was too afraid of losing you." And not having lost him, already she was thinking beyond him; had forgotten him, almost.

"No, Jen. No, you'd not have lost me, no matter what." He kissed her. That he was all-powerful, invulnerable, an Achilles with metaled heels was a fiction they would both maintain. She had built their marriage on it.

"This child. Your little girl." He frowned earnestly at her. "Surely you see that we can't get her back—"

"We can, Joel! We can!" She rose up from her knees and seated herself beside him on the sofa. "You see, I never signed the adoption papers. I refused. Legally, I'm still her mother."

"You just gave them the child? Like that?"

"Yes. I *couldn't* sign away my right to her." She studied her fingernails. "At least you've got to give me credit for that much, that I couldn't bring myself to give her away forever. Couldn't, just couldn't sign.

He pressed her hand. "Yes, I can imagine how you must have felt." He was silent—thinking. "You have papers? To prove she's—"

"Oh, yes. There's her birth certificate—Gil has a copy, and so have I. Then there would be the hospital records, and if necessary I can ask the doctor to write a letter. Besides, Gil's a lawyer; he knows I have every right to her. He'd never think of denying it."

"But we can't ask for her back right now, Jeanette.

Surely—"

Her eyes opened wide. "You don't want Margaret?"

He tried to smile, but the result was a little awkward. "Well, I haven't seen her, have I. Though I imagine I'll want her so long as you do. But not now, with this murder! The police are looking high and low for someone who could have killed your cousin's wife; for someone with a *reason* to have killed her . . ."

She sat quite still. "But, Joel. When I never thought of coming forward and making application for Margaret's return until I read that Enid had been killed—"

"How would the police know that was true? If you had gone to Enid earlier, you see, in an attempt to gain custody. They could see it that way: a violent disagreement over the child . . ."

Jeanette felt herself growing rigid, as if she were made of iron bars welded together. "But I didn't." Her voice was low and thick. "I didn't go to see Enid. I haven't seen her since the day she left the hospital in Minneapolis, taking my baby. Not since then."

He enclosed both her hands tightly in his. "Of course you haven't, Jen. I know that. I'm only saying how it might look. I'm only saying 'wait.' I'll talk to Roger Belden; he'll know what should be done, and when. We'll do this very legally."

She smiled, and the tenseness went out of her.

"Not a nice thing to do to your cousin Gil," he added.

"But it was a risk he took, in keeping her when I wouldn't sign any papers; he's a lawyer, he knew that. Besides, what's he going to do with her now, get a housekeeper? A girl that age needs a mother . . ." And more softly, *"Her* mother."

Chapter 6

THE FUNERAL was scheduled for early afternoon, on Friday. Beth Towse, that morning, sat in the kitchen of Phyll Strothers' house, talking, over coffee, with her late friend's sister. She had come over in order to bring her personal contribution to the sad occasion—a cake and a large, clove-studded ham.

"No, Gil's mother couldn't come," Phyll explained. "Her arthritis is too bad. But there'll be a few relatives from out of town—none staying over."

"What are the police doing? Do they think that man they arrested in Chicago—"

"They don't confide in me. But from the way Lieutenant Hogg questioned me yesterday afternoon, I wouldn't be surprised he thinks *I* did away with Enid."

Phyllis Strothers hadn't the slightest idea, actually, that what had set Orin Hogg against her was her own aggressive attitude. He suspected her of nothing worse than dyeing her raven tresses, but the Women's Lib edge to which she had honed her tongue had made him wary and, therefore, suspicious-seeming.

"You're kidding, of course," said Beth. "That man who confessed—Lemseider—"

"Yes, but if he *wasn't* the one . . . There are all kinds of crackpots, after all, who'll confess to things they never did. I still can't help wondering, in the light of—well, did Enid talk to you about her marital—well, you *did* know, didn't you, Beth?"

"You mean Barbara Dresser." Beth had wondered a great deal about this; there had been those little poisonous remarks Enid had made about Barbara, but no concrete information.

Quite deliberately Phyll set down her coffee cup. "Yes. There's no harm in talking about it now that she's—now that she's gone. I've had inside information from some time back that Barbara's been carrying on with Gil—who knows for how long. And, believe me, if it begins to look as if there was any connection between *that* grubby little business and my sister's death, I won't hesitate to tell the police exactly what I know . . ."

As a matter of fact, Phyll's cognizance of Barbara Dresser as a scarlet woman had been augmented only a few days ago when she'd discovered that Gil's secretary had been trying to capture Sidney Strait in her toils. Phyll had gone into the library to post on its bulletin board a notice about a Women's Lib lecture, and had had such an intelligent conversation with Mr. Strait, beginning when she had pointed out to him —though in friendly fashion—that the job he held was one traditionally filled by a female.

"I hope you don't feel," he had said, "that I've preempted a position that should have gone to some deserving woman. My viewpoint on that, you see, is much the same as yours: why should I be discriminated against on a purely sex basis, if I'm qualified for the job? Your gripe exactly, isn't it?"

"Partly. The other part, Mr. Strait, is this. I'll bet you're being paid more than Mrs. Semple ever was—for the same job."

"Inflation?" He smiled nicely.

"No, sex."

How had they gotten around to Barbara Dresser? Oh, yes—your brother-in-law's secretary, he'd said; apparently he'd picked up the family connection between Phyllis and the Weirs. Miss Dresser had seemed like a pleasant sort of girl, he'd remarked.

"Well, if you like *that* kind of girl." With the lift of an eyebrow she'd made sure he knew what she meant.

"Oh, really?" He had reddened, and she knew he understood. She'd fixed little Miss Barbara, all right. That had been before Enid had been killed, of course. She wouldn't hesitate, now, to nail Barbara's hide to the barn door, so to speak, for good and all . . .

Beth Towse left the house an hour later, after their tête-à-tête, thinking what a nice person Phyll Strothers really was. Strange that they had never become friends. Just one of those things. She couldn't imagine why it was she'd never liked Phyll.

And Phyll would have been delighted, had she known just how worried Barbara Dresser was—for fear the police investigation would turn up something about her imaginary liaison with Gil. Because Henrietta had talked, hadn't she? That was why Enid had become so suspicious? It was inconceivable, of course, that Gil actually could have killed his wife. But if the police thought he might have; or that the man up in Chicago was a hired assassin? Hired by Gil?

The eternal triangle; Barbara Dresser, the "other woman"; *bang,* you're dead . . .

She was developing a bad case of the jitters.

Before the services that afternoon, Orin Hogg called Gil to inform him that the self-confessed killer in Chicago, Clark Lemseider, was looking good as a suspect. He'd been able to draw a fair plan of most of the house and describe some of the furniture and even some of the wallpaper. Specifically he mentioned the grandfather's clock in the vestibule, and the little antique clock of Enid's, in the master bedroom. "Described that one in detail," said Orin. "The cupids and all. He seems to be a clock man."

The thought of a stranger standing uninvited in his bedroom was disturbing to Gil. No doubt, was there, that at some time or other the man had been there.

"I've got to be certain, though, Gil, before I initiate extradition proceedings; certain that Lemseider did kill your wife. I'll keep you posted."

And so the funeral services for Enid Weir were conducted during a rather confident lull in the investigation of her murder, with no visible cloud of suspicion hanging over any of those attending.

The three of them stood in Phyll's living room among the disorder of crumpled napkins, emptied coffee cups, and crumbed and chocolate-smeared dessert plates. The funeral and interment were over, and the last of Gil's relatives, and a solitary couple from Akron who were friends of Enid's and Phyll's, had finally left after stopping in for a collation.

A sense of things past and done with lingered in the air—the awareness of life not finished but put out, as surely as the butts of cigarettes that lay dead in the ashtrays. The stale smell of tobacco smoke combined depressingly with a sense of anticlimax.

"Of course Maggie's coming home with me." Gil frowned at his sister-in-law and slid an arm around Maggie's shoulders.

Phyllis's eyes were snappish. "It's no place for her to be—not after what's happened."

"She's coming with me." Gil's eyes were snappish in return. "It's the weekend. I'll be at home, with plenty of time to spend with her."

Phyll knew she was defeated; she had no actual grounds for keeping Gil from his adopted daughter. "Maybe for the weekend, then," she said grudgingly. "Till Sunday night?"

But when the two of them got home it was even more dismal than he'd expected. A pall seemed to hang over the empty rooms, like the presence, rather than the absence, of something.

It was a relief when the phone rang—and like summer in

November to hear Cinny's voice. "I hope you don't mind my calling, Gil." Mind? How could he mind? "Trina wants to have Maggie over for the night. I thought I'd ask you first . . ."

And so it was that he stood, a few minutes before six, at the Howland front door with his daughter's overnight case in his hand. Maggie ducked inside the moment Trina opened the door, leaving him face to face with Cinny on the doorsill.

"I'd better not come in . . ." he said tentatively.

"No."

And he was at once aware, at his back, of the houses on the street, their lighted windows like so many eyes staring out at whoever came and went.

Inside, of course, would be Miss Lucille Howland; there would be no privacy in which he and Ted Howland's widow could talk. And it was too soon, anyhow—even for talk.

Cinny was wearing gray slacks and a jewel-toned green plush top. She couldn't have looked lovelier in a ball gown.

"Have you made up your mind about the Fenton place?" he asked.

"Yes. I gave Mrs. Fenton a binder on it this morning."

He nodded, relieved that she was staying on. "Would you like me to handle it for you?"

"Yes, if you will."

"Good. I'll give Mrs. Fenton a call." That was what he said, but not what he wanted to say. How could you tell the girl you loved how you felt about her when the wife you had also loved—or thought you did, for a good number of years —had been lowered into the earth and covered over with dirt and sod only three hours before?

He handed her Maggie's case.

"I'll bring her home tomorrow, Gil."

"O.K. And—I'll be calling you, Cinny." As he turned away he felt defeated—by the impossibility of communicating to her what he wanted to; by her cool impersonality (a safeguard, for them both?); by public opinion.

He went on down the walk to his car.

No real obstacle between them, anymore . . . Only the whole town of Selkirk.

Chapter 7

ALTHOUGH HE was busy that following week with various matters he'd been working on for some time past, Gil could not help but be aware of a certain slacking off of calls requesting him to undertake the handling of newly arisen problems. Merely coincidence? Or people hesitating to bother him when he was presumably still adjusting to a personal tragedy? Or was it something more?

At Rotary, one of the younger lawyers in town went out of his way to let him know that two or three of Gil's old clients had come to him this week with their legal work . . . A trend? . . . Perhaps people weren't sure, after all, that the police had the right man up in Chicago.

And what was Orin doing about that, anyway—still finagling with the State of Illinois over the matter of extradition?

And Barbara—his own secretary—was afraid of him, he thought. He couldn't help noticing . . .

It was on Friday that Orin Hogg called and asked if Gil could come over to his office.

"Afraid I've got some disappointing news," Selkirk's detective-lieutenant greeted him with on his arrival. "We've lost our suspect."

"Lemseider?"

"Yes, Lemseider. Illinois gets to keep him. In digging into his background, we discovered that Lemseider was living just outside Selkirk a couple of years ago, staying with an uncle—an old farmer who's since died. Clark Lemseider worked for several months during that period as a paper hanger, assisting Charlie Koonts here in town."

"Oh." One sentence had made it all clear.

"Yeah. Lemseider helped hang the paper in your house when your wife redecorated. No wonder he could tell the detectives in Chicago all about the inside. The murder details were just guesswork for him, and he guessed a couple things right, and one or two wrong—though you expect that, in the heat of the moment, no one can remember everything just the way it happened. Anyhow, he's been definitely placed in Chicago, now, during the afternoon of the murder."

"Well. The end of that. Does he admit he made up the whole—?"

"Now he does—yes."

"Why? Did he say why he claimed—"

"Oh, that's easy enough. He wanted to move a little higher up in the penitentiary pecking order. Delusions of grandeur. He saw the account of the murder in the paper just before they picked him up, and I guess that gave him the idea."

"So now what, O.H.?"

Orin sighed wearily. "Pretty cold trail by this time. I've been following up everything I could, but not much has come my way. You got any fresh inspiration on the subject, Gil?"

"No." The face of his wife was suddenly before him again, with the bullet hole in the forehead. He closed his eyes, but the picture only became clearer, and he opened them once more.

She shouldn't watch such a scary program, she guessed. With a glance over her shoulder at the black oblong that was the nearest window, Barbara got up from her chair and switched channels.

She wished that the drapes were the kind that drew over the windows. They could be pulled partway over the glass, but nowhere near meeting, and that was worse, because partly drawn they would give protection to anyone looking in from outside. No: if they could see in, she'd rather be able to see out, in case anybody *was* there. Though of course nobody was.

It was the murder that had made her so nervous; so fearful. She never used to imagine shadowy figures waiting in the dark of the closets, anonymous forms huddled in the empty rooms of the house, even faceless men hiding under the beds. But the thought of someone stealing into the Weir house came to her constantly now, when she was alone. Because Enid had been alone. Had he been waiting for her somewhere inside, behind something, when she came home from the grocery or some other errand? Or had he soundlessly opened the door and crept in when she was already there? Barbara shivered, and tried to focus her attention wholly on the domestic comedy, with its canned laughter, emanating from the T.V.

Yet he mightn't have sneaked into the house at all. Maybe he had come boldly through the front door, admitted by Enid herself. Since it wasn't the man i·· Chicago, the one who'd confessed—and she wished now that she hadn't even seen the evening paper with *that* news—since it wasn't, now, it could have been someone Enid knew, who'd killed her. Someone here in Selkirk, more than likely. Certainly not Gil. But someone here . . . Who? Someone who was still here.

Another glance over the shoulder.

And she drew in a breath and almost strangled on it. For an endless moment her eyes were glued to the rectangle of night, where a face stared back at her.

And then it was gone.

The breath she had strangled on turned into a sort of hiccup, and she made her way stumblingly to the phone and called the police.

Gil spent half of Saturday morning trying to calm down Barbara Dresser.

"But the police didn't find a trace of anyone, Barbara."

"That doesn't prove he wasn't there. I saw him!"

Barbara had apparently had a Peeping Tom at one of her windows.

And she was right—the fact that the police hadn't nabbed him didn't mean he hadn't been there.

For himself, Gil wondered what the police were doing about something other than Barbara's elusive and perhaps illusory visitor: Enid's murder. Now that Orin had lost his suspect . . .

Saturday night Maggie was slated to go to a pajama party, and Gil dropped her off. "Trina invited too?" he had asked earlier, and had been assured she was.

He lingered, watching his daughter safely up to the house, wondering whether Trina had already been delivered to the party. His heart gave a skip and a thud as he recognized Cinny's car pulling up behind his.

He left the engine running and got out, timing his maneuver carefully so that he reached the window of her car just as Trina went flying up the walk to overtake Maggie at the door.

He rapped on the glass and she lowered it.

"Hello, Gil."

He just stood there, warmed by her presence so near him.

"Cinny, I've got to see you."

"You are seeing me."

"I mean I've got to talk to you."

"I don't know how you can, really. Except on the phone? You're the one who pointed out about the gossip and all . . ."

"Yes, I know. Look—could you have dinner with me tonight?"

"Dinner? That *would* start talk. I can hear it now."

"Not here. Out of town. We can drive till we find someplace."

"I don't know, Gil . . ." She looked troubled.

He put his hand through the open window and touched

hers, on the steering wheel. Even through gloves the contact was rewarding. "It's important," he said.

"All right."

It was quickly arranged, and a few minutes later he pulled into the alley behind Miss Howland's house, watched Cinny put her car away in the garage, and as she came through the little gate in the fence by the trash cans, he opened the car door for her from inside.

"Sorry to be so clandestine," he said.

"I feel as if we were on our way to rob a bank, at *least.*"

"Yet there's nothing wrong with our seeing each other. *Nothing.*"

"Not now—no."

No, not now. His thought echoed hers.

"At least I didn't have to explain anything to Aunt Lucille. She's gone to bed early, with a cold." Cinny was apparently still mulling over whether she should have come.

He drove to Kokomo—to the far side. Selected a motel with a restaurant—one of a chain which advertised its gourmet food.

"Should be all right," he said to Cinny. He didn't know a living soul in Kokomo, and was sure Cinny didn't either.

The restaurant was cozy—and dark; you had almost to feel your way to a table. Dark walls, red carpet, red upholstery, red tablecloths; a heavy, ornate fireplace in which danced the red and orange light of an imitation log fire.

"It seems strange, being with you," she said over their first drink. "And in this place—" She gestured. "Like another world."

"Cinny, you know why I wanted to see you."

"Supposing you tell me, though. I don't know how you're going to put it."

The truth was that he didn't know either. He poked with the little plastic stir at the ice over which his martini had been poured. "That day out at the Fenton place," he began. "I never experienced anything like it in my life. I've always thought I ran my own life, made my own decisions—master of my fate, captain of my soul. Not *that* day. Believe me, I had no intention of touching you, of making any kind of pitch; and then all of a sudden there we were, touching, and you were the only thing in the world that mattered. Nothing I could do about it."

"That's bothered me a great deal, Gil. That afternoon. I can't get rid of the idea that I was kissing you at the very time your wife was being shot to death. It makes me feel— not nice; as if I'd put a hex on her and she died because of it."

"Oh, my lord! That's utter nonsense. That's your Puritan conscience trying to punish you for something over which you had no control. *I* kissed *you*—you had nothing to do with it."

"Didn't I?"

"No. And none of it had anything to do with Enid. Certainly it didn't bring about her death, it didn't even cause her a moment of unhappiness."

"Only because she died. If she hadn't, who knows—?"

"Cinny, dear, listen to me. Things began going wrong between Enid and me before you came here. Quite wrong. We— Oh, hell, why do I have to apologize for being in love with you! Something I obviously never grew out of. I had only to see you again and . . . Cinny, will you marry me? When a decent amount of time has elapsed?"

It seemed forever that he was poised between heaven and hell, not knowing which it was to be . . . . He had asked too soon; and he should have waited until she was weakened by physical contact, overwhelmed by her own chemistry as they clung together, somewhere, in the darkness—somewhere else, not here in a public restaurant.

After an eternity, she answered.

"Probably," she said. "I suppose I won't be able to help myself."

"I hope not." The grin on his face felt wonderful.

"Trina will have to approve . . ."

"I don't think that'll be too much of an obstacle. Do you? Lucky that Maggie and Trina are such good friends."

They held hands, between courses. Afterward Gil couldn't remember anything about his steak—good or indifferent.

Over coffee she was thoughtful. "I wish they'd find someone to arrest for her murder, and get it over with."

"Yes . . . Only I sometimes wonder whether we'd all be better off—not knowing."

"Yes—there's that. No evidence of robbery, was there . . ."

"Except that my revolver's missing."

She looked up quickly. "Oh. I didn't know that, Gil."

"But I have no way of knowing whether it was taken then or earlier."

The shadow of worry in her amber eyes. "That's—kind of nervous-making, isn't it. Could it have been the gun that was used?"

"It could well have been. She was killed with a thirty-two caliber; that's what mine was—a thirty-two."

She touched his wrist with her fingers. "I wish you had let me tell the police that you were with *me* when she was murdered."

He smiled a little wryly. "You left me before three-thirty, a I recall. Like maybe twenty after three. I'd still have had time to drive home after that and quarrel with her and—shoot her dead; and be gone again before Beth Towse arrived a few minutes after four."

"Oh. Can't you prove you were somewhere—"

"I can't prove anything. I was all by myself. Thinking."

"Where?"

"In the woods back of Fentons' barn. I took a walk, and sat down on a fallen tree. Tried to piece my life together again without you; I didn't do very well." The desperation of that afternoon, remembered now, started forth his desire like a spurred horse. He wanted her in his arms—now; now

72

that it was possible. "Let's get out of here, shall we?" His voice was so husky he scarcely recognized it as his own.

Once safe among the rows of cars—no one, at the moment, was coming in or out of the lot or the restaurant—Gil stopped and pulled her to him. He should never have proposed to her inside, where he couldn't take hold of her like this, take her lips, take all of her in his arms, feel her hair under his hand . . .

"Hey—" she interrupted him softly. "I'm not sure you know your own strength!"

"Sorry." He eased up, pressed his cheek to hers, held her gently with his hands against her shoulder blades. "It's been such a long, long time—"

In the car he pushed her coat back, hugged her beneath it. One button at a time he undid the top of her dress until she stopped him. But he slid one hand inside and held her closer. Long ago, she wouldn't have permitted such a thing —but since then she'd been married, they were adult now and it was different.

Little wonder, was it, that neither of them saw the blurred white face that watched them through the driver's window of an automobile parked opposite; had watched them embrace, out in the open, and peered now through the glass, trying to see from thirty feet away just what they were doing.

"We could take a room in the motel . . . ?" His lips against the base of her throat.

"No. No, I don't think so, Gil. Let's not."

When they drove out of the blacktopped lot a little later, the watcher in the occupied car took note of the direction in which they turned on the highway and a moment later started the engine. Yes, there they were, not far ahead; it was easy to keep them in sight, and the following car stayed well back on the return trip to Selkirk.

Chapter 8

ORIN HOGG leaned his six-foot-two frame against the circulation desk and waited for the little blond man coming toward him through the stacks.

"You asked to see me?"

"Yes. I'm Lieutenant Hogg—Police Department. I'd like to talk to you for a few minutes—"

"Of course," said Sidney Strait, trying not to look guilty —a look common to people Orin talked to, he knew it well. "In my office?" With conspicuous casualness the head librarian led the way—and shut the door after the two of them.

"Now. What can I do for you, Lieutenant?"

"It's about this Weir murder. I understand there was some kind of trouble between you and Mrs. Weir. Could you tell me about it?"

Strait's look was deprecating. "No killing matter, I can assure you. We had a couple of little arguments about some books she claimed she'd returned. She refused to pay for them, refused to pay the fines, and said I had accused her of dishonesty; I hadn't, of course, but—" He shrugged.

"Was that all?"

"That's all that *happened*. Yes. She may have said some unfriendly things about me, around town—I don't know."

"Surely you were aware that she was exerting pressure on some members of the library board in an attempt to oust you from your job?" He had stumbled upon this piece of information only yesterday.

"No. I didn't know that," Sidney Strait said slowly, looking him right in the eye. Digesting the information? Or guarding the fact that he *had* known?

"Why would she do that, Mr. Strait?"

"She didn't like me. The very first time we met, something—something unfortunate happened." He smiled, dryly. "Half the town was there—witnesses; surely you've heard about it? I mistook her for the elder Mrs. Weir, Mr. Weir's mother."

Orin was unable to suppress a smile. No killing matter? from whose point of view . . . "She must have been as mad as a hornet. I can imagine. Yet you didn't know she was taking steps against you?"

"I knew she had it in for me, was all. Nothing more specific."

Well, thought Orin, that could be so. No reason he would have known what she was doing behind his back. All the same, Orin decided, as he left the neat brick building with its quiet, orderly interior and started down the steps, he'd send some inquiries about Strait to Maybridge, Indiana, where he had lived before coming to Selkirk. There might be something in his background . . .

"Why can't I stay at Trina's? Instead of Aunt Phyllis's house?"

"Because it's up to your aunt to look after you, now that Mama isn't here anymore. That's what families are for."

Gil sat with his daughter in the Country Kitchen, a restaurant that had just opened in the new shopping center. They had escaped from Aunt Phyllis for the evening.

"But when I hate it there. Joyce treats me like I was a little kid—and she's only two years older than me. And I don't like how Benson is all the time . . ."

"How is that?"

"Always asking me questions. About Mom. About you."

"What kind of questions?"

"Oh, I don't know. Like he's trying to find out things."

"Well, the police are doing that too, everybody'd like to find out who killed your mother; I expect Benson's no exception."

"Sometimes he acts like he knows something. Like he knows a lot, really, that I don't, and that nobody else—"

"Oh, well, Benson's always like that. At seventeen he knows *everything*."

"Daddy," she said. "Daddy—"

She stopped and Gil looked at her and could see that something else was on her mind. Not just disliking it at Aunt Phyll's, not just Benson. "What is it, honey? Something wrong?"

He saw her swallow, and her lips parted. "Do you mind talking—about Mama? I mean about the day she was killed?"

"We haven't talked about that, really, have we. It won't upset me—any more than I have been all along. Ever since it happened. But I haven't talked about it to you because— well, I guess I thought the less said about how she died, the better for you. Maybe that was a mistake on my part?"

She gave a sort of gasp of relief. "Oh, that's how I've felt about you! And I guess I was wrong. You didn't know I was anywhere near home that day, did you, Daddy?"

His heart gave a thud. "You were at the house? The afternoon Mama—"

She shook her head quickly. "I walked past on the sidewalk on the way to Girl Scout meeting at Lisa's house."

"But that's not the way to Lisa's from school—"

"No, but Meegan had to get something from her house that she was supposed to bring to the meeting and she'd forgotten it. So we came down our street on the way. I didn't remember about it till just today—but I saw a car parked in front of the house."

"In front of *our* house?"

"Yes. No one was in it, but he could have been inside then."

"Yes, I suppose he could have."

"Shouldn't we tell the police? Now that I've remembered it?"

"Definitely. Why is it you didn't think of it till today?"

Her face was troubled. "I guess I just didn't want to think about any of it at all—anything that happened then."

Orin Hogg went out to Kennedy Junior High School. To check Maggie Weir's story.

It had been a gray car, she said, and she didn't know what make. New? Or old? Well, sort of old, she guessed; it didn't look like a this-year's model, or even last. License? Hadn't noticed.

Meegan Commiger, who had been with Maggie, had not seen the car. Though it could have been there; she hadn't noticed. She knew Maggie hadn't paid much attention either, because she'd never mentioned it till some of the kids started tormenting her about her father, and what would it be like to have a jailbird in the family; and Maggie had gone to the Girls' Room and cried. It had been after that that she'd remembered the gray car.

Orin reported to Gil on the matter, by phone. "These kids have been picking on your daughter, that's all. And as I see it, she's thought up something to try to help you out: she saw a car. Maybe she did, but it seems pretty insubstantial to me. You've got a nice daughter in your corner, Gil, I'll say that."

So much for the mysterious gray car.

Gil had a worried phone call at home one evening that week—from his mother, in Fort Lauderdale.

"How's the arthritis, Mother?"

"About the same, Gil. No better, no worse." He could see almost as clearly as if she were there with him, the short, carefully kept blue-gray hair framing the pinched, tanned face with its long pain lines running down the cheeks. "Gil —I'm upset. *Very* upset. I've been talking to Gladys Rice's mother—you know she's down here now, we're in the same bridge group. From what Gladys writes—well, are people around Selkirk saying *you* killed Enid?"

"Oh. Some gossip, maybe—haven't heard it, myself."

"But gossip like *that,* Gil! Why, we've never had a murder in Selkirk—"

"Exactly. The bridge players have never had anything quite that lurid to hash over. But they'll get over it."

"Will they, Gil? Oh, my! If the thing isn't solved—"

"It will be, I'm sure. The police are working on it still. And they certainly haven't arrested me, have they? Orin Hogg—you remember him—is in charge, and he's an old friend, you know that."

"It's not hurting your business?"

"No, no. Of course not."

It *was* hurting business. The office phone hardly rang anymore.

Orin Hogg heard from Maybridge, Indiana, that week. Nothing unfavorable was known there of Sidney Strait. He had been an excellent assistant librarian in the Maybridge Public Library. Single—he had led a quiet, unobtrusive existence, living in a furnished apartment downtown and being active in the Lutheran Church in Maybridge.

Orin filed the information away.

Gil phoned Cinny on Friday. "Dinner?" he asked. "Same arrangement as last time?"

"I'd love it, Gil. Only—"

"Only what?"

"Well, Trina will be gone on that Girl Scout campout—along with Maggie. But what do I tell Aunt Lucille?"

"Why not tell her the truth?"

"Well, yes. What a brilliant idea. She's not small-minded, and she's very sensible."

And so, under cover of darkness he called for Cinny at

Miss Howland's front door. It seemed so nice, so normal. And she told him how much better it made her feel not to have lied to Aunt Lucille.

"There's no reason you shouldn't see me," Gil said—wishing he could believe it.

At dinner—the same motel, in Kokomo—his eyes roved over the dark red scene and the ersatz pyrotechnics of the imitation log fire. There was a large stain on the carpet beside their table, and grease splattered on the flocked wallpaper at Cinny's elbow.

He met her thoughtful gaze. "I'd never have supposed something like this would become 'our place,' but it seems to have."

"It's great. I like it."

"So do I."

The watcher in the car outside scrunched down into his seat as they emerged from the restaurant; followed their progress, arm in arm, to Gil's car; waited as they stood talking on the asphalt paving. As on the other occasion, he took her in his arms, they kissed. And they talked some more. They got into the car then, and Gil started the engine. But instead of heading out onto the highway, he turned into the drive in front of the motel.

The watcher smiled. Fascinated.

"Gil . . ." she was saying hesitantly as he parked again, in front of the motel office. "I'm afraid this is very rash . . ."

"Then let's do it. Before we're too old to do anything rash." His lips on hers again. "I love you."

"All right," she whispered, and he got out of the car and went into the motel office. She had known, hadn't she, that when she'd said yes to dinner this time she'd say yes later to this.

It was the following Monday afternoon that Orin Hogg stopped Gil in the main corridor of the City Building just as court was about to reconvene after the lunch break.

"I want to talk to you, Gil."

"When I'm through here? I'm going into court right now."

So midafternoon, when he had gotten Rod Black's boy off with a suspended sentence, he dropped by Orin's office.

"Just wanted to bring a few things up to date—concerning the death of your wife." The tall redhead looked up at him from behind the desk and motioned Gil to a chair.

"You've turned up something new?"

"Well, yes. A motive, possibly."

"For whom?"

"For you. All this time that we've both lived in this town I never realized you were such a womanizer."

Gil felt his face set quite rigidly. "Womanizer? I'm not."

"First there was this story—though it reached me only recently—about you and Barbara Dresser."

"There's *nothing* going on between Barbara Dresser and me!"

O.H. lifted an eyebrow; lowered it. "But now it's not Barbara; is it. It's Cynthia Howland. Ever since she came back to town."

"You know I won't do anything but deny that," Gil said angrily. "And Cynthia Howland would never be a party to—"

"Oh, wouldn't she? I know for a fact that you and Mrs. Howland shared a room in a motel in Kokomo on Friday night."

Gil's rage was red-hot. "You mean you've had a *tail* on me?"

O.H. shook his head. "The information was a pure gift. Someone saw you there."

"You'll have to prove it, of course—"

"No problem. My informant will be happy to testify, if need be. And we have this." From a drawer of his desk he took a card and laid it before Gil. God! Orin had wasted no time. It was the registration card he'd made out at the motel.

" 'Mr. and Mrs. Mason,' I see, who enjoyed the hospitality up there in Kokomo. But a handwriting expert can—"

"O.K. You needn't go on. But look—just who is this informant who will be so happy to testify? What's *his* stake in this case? Because he has one, I'm sure! This is no chance piece of information, it's something your source went to trouble to get, for a *reason*. Who is it?"

"I can't tell you that. But it's fairly evident, isn't it, that you're hardly pining away with grief for your wife, when barely two weeks after—"

"You can cut the lecture, Orin. If you're trying to point out that I'm an unfeeling bastard, you're wrong. I couldn't have been married to Enid for twenty years and not find her death a terrible shock—something that takes a lot of getting used to. At the same time, this wasn't Romeo and Juliet— a lot can go out of a relationship, too, in two decades. But if you feel a man shouldn't be able to forget too easily a woman he's loved, you're right. I haven't forgotten my wife, and I never will. But I also never forgot Cynthia Neiswanner. I would have married her, you know, if she hadn't gone off and married Ted Howland. Now that she's back and we're both free . . ."

"That's not the sequence, according to the information I have. You had resumed things with Cynthia *before* your wife's death—a fact you've been concealing. For instance when you told me you went alone to the Fenton place to look it over, that wasn't true. I've located someone who saw Cynthia Howland there that afternoon. You wouldn't have bothered to lie about her presence at the farm with you, if something hadn't been going on between the two of you— if it had been an ordinary lawyer-client relationship.

"And don't count on her for an alibi. She was recognized by a Selkirk teacher, a very responsible person who observed her leaving at some time before three-thirty. A man was standing in the drive by the house as she drove away; that would have been you. Before three-thirty? You still had time after—"

"Yes," Gil cut in. "I follow your train of thought. Why tell me all this, instead of saving it to clobber me with at my trial?"

"Because there isn't a good enough case against you to be *sure* of getting a conviction for murder. It's all circumstantial . . . There's one other little piece of testimony—" Orin broke off and studied Gil—thinking, apparently. "By what route did you get to the McCutcheon farm that afternoon, from the Fenton place?"

The question was loaded—Gil knew that. He could see the challenge in the lieutenant's nice blue eyes, in the nice friendly face he had known all his life. Orin's old nickname, the one that had plagued him all through grade school, floated through his mind. Oinky. Oinky Hogg, pronounced Hog. But the recollection added no humor to the situation; the runty bricktopped kid he'd scuffled with on a long-ago playground wasn't Oinky now, he was a very capable police lieutenant who was building piece by piece a serviceable murder case against one Gilman Weir, hapless attorney.

Somehow, on this question, O.H. was expecting to prove him a liar. Gil took a deep breath and plunged. "I came through the edge of town. Took Forty-seven in as far as Dunlop Street, turned onto that and followed it south out of Selkirk as far as Liberty Road and cut across on that to Route Thirty-one."

"You were in the southwest sector of town, in other words?"

"That's right."

"You didn't go in as far as, say, Walnut Street?"

"No."

"What if I were to tell you you were seen *east* of Walnut, not more than three blocks from your home and heading in that direction?"

Gil paused, wary. "You said *'what if.'* Are you saying someone did claim to see me in that part of town?"

"Yes. Someone did."

"I went home to lunch that day—sure *that* wasn't when I was spotted?"

"No. It was a little before four o'clock."

A nightmare feeling of unreality had been creeping over Gil during this exchange. "Whoever told you he saw me then is lying. I wasn't there—not at that time."

Orin shrugged. "It'll be up to the jury, won't it, to decide who's lying. Because you see, there is a case against you; circumstantial, but we may have to use it just as it is. Motive: you were having an affair with another woman, whom you presumably intend to marry; and I've had no trouble finding people who tell me you and your wife were not getting along. Opportunity: you were seen in the neighborhood of your home, going in that direction, only a short time before she was found dead. Means: your thirty-two revolver is missing, and she was killed with a thirty-two. Additional point: your attempt to set up an alibi. Isn't it evident that you could reasonably have expected Mrs. McCutcheon to alibi you? Because she's very forgetful, you could have counted on her to say you'd been at her house; and you *would* have been, and she wouldn't have been sure what time you got there or what time you left. Coupled with your secretary's testimony that you left the office intending to go straight there, Mrs. McCutcheon's account of your visit could have been made to seem plausibly to cover the time you were somewhere else. Unfortunately for you, your wife's body was discovered too soon and I phoned Mrs. McCutcheon before you'd even arrived."

"Are you trying to frighten me? I can see the case you've got, you don't have to—"

"I'm telling you I don't like the case—too circumstantial. But the prosecutor will go into court with it if it's all we've got. The reason I'm outlining it for you is that I'm sure you don't want Cynthia Howland undressed in court—which is what it'll amount to, with that bit about the motel. She'd be humiliated, her little girl would be hurt—and you know this town: you'd never be able to practice law here in any comfort even if you got off. That what you want?"

"Do you need to ask?" Gil said, very low. "What is it you want, then, to call it off?"

"That's pretty obvious. If you killed your wife, quit stalling and plead guilty. There'd be no question of first degree murder—I can't, actually, imagine your planning a thing like that. I believed you, for instance, when you told me that you ran into Cynthia after you'd told Barbara you were going to McCutcheons', and changed your plans and went to the Fenton farm instead. But I also think it very likely that after some kind of talk with Cynthia that day you went home to have it out with your wife about a divorce. Which is just the kind of argument that can become heated and possibly hysterical; for all I know, your wife threatened suicide if you left her and you tried to stop her. We do know, for instance, that she was shot at close range. You might get by with a manslaughter plea . . ."

"I'm not going to confess to something I didn't do."

"So you'll let this go into court? With the motel testimony—"

"I think you're bluffing. I don't thing Bill Martin will prosecute on such circumstantial evidence."

"Your risk. And you've got to admit I'm being more than fair. How many murder suspects are given a preview of the prosecution's case?"

"Are you arresting me?"

"Not as of the moment. I'd like to have a tighter case, as I say. So, hoping I can nail down a few more details . . ."

"I still think you're bluffing."

Orin looked quizzically at him. "We'll see. And don't leave town."

Gil left the City Building for the walk back to his own office in a deepening feeling of unreality. It wasn't possible for things to have gone so wrong. Rash, he kept thinking;

Cinny had said it was rash, the motel. My, hadn't it been! Someone must have followed them there. Such a thing had not occurred to him, as he knew O.H., with the small-town police force that was all he had to work with, hadn't the manpower to undertake much surveillance. Who, then? And who had claimed to have seen him near home the afternoon of Enid's death? Who could possibly . . .

He nodded, or smiled, at people he knew as they passed him on the sidewalk; caught the look of speculation in this face or that one; felt from behind him the over-the-shoulder glance; sensed the question that had inevitably risen to mind at sight of him: Had he murdered his wife?

The blow that fell when he got back to his office and to the mail that had arrived this morning while he was in court was totally unexpected—like being poleaxed from the rear while watching the enemies ranged in front of him. It was in a letter from an Indianapolis law firm, and the signature was that of an attorney well known to anyone in this part of the state who ever read a newspaper. Roger Belden.

He read the letter and felt as though the life were being squeezed out of him.

He went back a second time to the last paragraph.

I am sure you are fully cognizant, as a lawyer, that since no adoption proceedings were ever undertaken, the claim of the natural parent has never been terminated. Mrs. Davis's right to the child thus takes legal precedence over any other claim whatsoever. I hope that with this in mind you will see that the best interests of all concerned can be served only by your full cooperation.

The thing he had feared all these years. Jeanette wanted Maggie back.

Chapter 9

ROGER BELDEN had moved fast. Gil had received the letter on Monday, and here it was only Wednesday and Jeanette's lawyer had managed to get the hearing for custody of Maggie crowded onto Judge Clement Owsler's calendar for the afternoon—squeezed in before the Thanksgiving weekend. Money, Gil suspected, must have greased the wheels somewhere or other.

Gil, too, had moved fast, lining up Maggie's pediatrician as an expert witness and in addition snagging a psychiatrist from Indianapolis to give an opinion at the hearing.

For all the good it would do . . .

The look of his daughter when Gil had told her about the proceedings that had been set in motion by her real mother was something he would have preferred to forget.

"How can she, Daddy? I thought adopted was something you couldn't change back."

He had tried to explain. "She couldn't bring herself to give you away irrevocably," he finished. "She refused to sign the papers." Cooperating, am I not, he thought bitterly, as Roger Belden asked me to—which meant not trying to turn the child against the mother who had given her up to someone else to raise.

"But I don't want to go with her!"

"I don't want you to, either. You know that! We'll do everything we can . . ."

Cinny had been appalled. He'd phoned her on Monday,

with the debris of his life still settling round him after the detonation of Jeanette's time bomb. (Which he'd known, always, was there; he just hadn't known whether or not it was a dud. It certainly hadn't been.)

"Oh, Gil! That's unbelievable!" But then Cinny had been unaware, until just now, of the circumstances.

"Unbelievable? Afraid not."

"Legally, I suppose she can . . ."

"Yes. Especially since at this point I don't look too good. Murderers make unfit fathers, wouldn't you say?" No need, with Cinny, for the careful public mask, the bland assumption of non-guilt. (Just *once* look slightly guilty and already he would be convicted in the mind of any possible juror who could be impaneled in Selkirk.)

"Gil, don't! Don't say things like that!"

There was something else, too, that he must break to Cinny. After filling her in a little more on Maggie, he got around to it.

"Cin, I hate to tell you this . . . Orin Hogg knows about the motel business Saturday night."

"Oh." There was a short silence while she presumably analyzed the information. "We were—followed?"

"Not by anyone on the Selkirk Police Department payroll, according to Orin. Someone else. You didn't notice any-one—"

"No. No, I didn't. Gil—does this put you in deeper? In case Orin is thinking—"

"Oh, don't worry about me." He tried to sound only cynical, not worried; oh, certainly he mustn't sound worried. "My own damn fault, too. But it's on your account I mind. Cin, I can't tell you how sorry I am. I shouldn't have insisted. If—"

"And I shouldn't have said yes, should I! I can't regret it, Gil—and if you say you do, I'll never speak to you again."

He wouldn't have supposed he'd be able to smile. But he smiled.

By the time he'd hung up, the smile had died. He wouldn't be seeing her now—for how long? Not even on the Q.T., since perhaps they were still being spied on . . . His life had narrowed down to one thing only. A fight, alone, to keep Maggie.

With what kind of odds?

And already it was Wednesday, now. They were gathered in the Judge's chambers for the hearing—the adults only, at first, with Maggie waiting in an office down the hall in the company of her Aunt Phyll.

They had spoken—he and Jeanette—a bare acknowledgment; and Joel Davis had introduced himself. Gil would have recognized him from his pictures—a beefy, handsome man in an expensive blue-black suit. The heir to the Davis holdings. Between Gil and the Davises sat their attorney, Roger Belden—a very slick, knowledgeable operator. Belden had made his reputation years ago as counsel for the first Joel Davis, whose various business coups had landed the two of them in the public eye and the public prints over and over again.

"Well, now." Judge Owsler cleared his throat. "This is a preliminary hearing. Any conclusions reached today will be tentative only, to be reviewed at a later date which I'll decide on as I see fit." He glanced around at those assembled, ending with a special little nod for Gil. Years spent working in court in one another's company had added mutual respect to mutual liking.

"This matter has been hurried along"—the Judge's glance rested here on Jeanette's lawyer—"by Mr. Belden, acting as attorney for Mrs. Davis. I understand, Mrs. Davis, that you are worried about the uncertain conditions under which the child, Margaret, is living as a result of her foster mother's death." (Not money, then, that had hastened these proceedings, but expediency decked out in hearts and flowers.)

Jeanette framed a soundless "yes" in a quivering smile and

lowered her eyes.

They went over the documents, then, that were in the Judge's possession. Sallow-faced, squirrel-cheeked, Clem Owsler, with his thatch of prematurely white hair, studied all the papers. He looked over the top of his half-glasses at Gil. "But I believe that in any case you do not deny Mrs. Davis's contention that she is the child's natural mother?"

"No," said Gil.

"Nor was any adoption procedure initiated, at any time—"

"No, it was not."

"Then can you show cause why Margaret Weir should not be given into her mother's custody, now that the request has been made?"

"I can." Gil swallowed, trying to choke down his rising emotion.

He began. "This is not a case, Your Honor, of an infant being reclaimed by a parent who has changed her mind. Margaret is twelve. She has known no home but the one she has grown up in; no parents but my wife Enid and myself. To uproot her at this stage in her life would surely do her great emotional and psychological harm."

Roger Belden sat with a little smile, listening. Confident. A tall man, graying, hair parted in the middle above the mahogany-hued forehead of the perennial golfer.

"If I may call expert witnesses to give testimony—"

First Dr. Nelson Cruse—plump, balding, with a grumpy, sometimes even ferocious manner, which failed to deceive even his youngest patients.

"This child has been my patient since she was ten days old," Dr. Cruse rasped accusingly, as though she had done him some unforgivable injury. "I remember the first visit she made to my office. Tiny little thing, squalling her head off. The Weirs had just brought her home from Minneapolis." He shot an angry look at Gil. "Good parents, Gil and his wife—took *extra* care of Maggie, partly I expect because they'd waited so long for a baby."

Gil listened. Kind words, all, from the doctor, seemingly torn from him against his will. Toward the end of his rather rambling testimony, as he summarized his reasons for opposing the removal of Maggie from her home in Selkirk, his manner softened.

"And these good people"—he looked almost benevolently at the two Davises, the effect being almost like a blessing from Satan—"for their own ego-satisfaction are willing to entirely disrupt the life of this child, Maggie Weir?"

Jeanette stirred uneasily, Joel Davis frowned into the distance, and Roger Belden's face remained quite expressionless. Gil was sure Belden had not cared either for what Nelson Cruse had said or for his style of delivery.

Dr. Milton Gorse next; the psychiatrist. Slight, frail-looking, hardly filling out his clothes; a youngish man, with thick curly hair, thin lips, and glasses. He addressed himself directly to the Judge.

"My personal acquaintanceship with the child in this case consists of a short conversation I had with her about half an hour ago. Yet even from that I'd say I know a fair amount about her. What I have to say, however, comes mostly from my experience in dealing with many children who have suffered painful transplantings—and children, you know, more than anyone else, distrust change, resist it. Children are the classic conservatives among us: they wish things to remain always the same. These transplantings, then, whether occasioned by death, or illness in the family, or by legal intervention in cases of parental cruelty or neglect . . ."

Dr. Gorse's testimony was all that Gil could have wished.

Roger Belden remained impassive. And it was Belden who asked, when the medical testimony was finished, whether Dr. Gorse could stay on a bit. "I may have some questions for him later on." Gil realized suddenly why it was that the attorney reminded him of a turtle; it was the loose flesh hanging down from the jawbone, so that the chin sloped away into his neck without any defining line. Just so had a long-ago pet turtle of

Maggie's looked, on spotting a dead fly afloat in the tank, puffing out its neck preparatory to drawing back the wicked reptile head for an all-inclusive bite.

Dr. Cruse glanced inquiringly about, brows knit in a frown, lips drawn up in a grim smile. "If there's no further need for me—"

There had hardly been a need for the question; his departure could not come too soon for Jeanette's attorney, as was evident from the disapproval with which his eyes raked the doctor, and the annoyed shake of his head.

When he had gone, the Judge nodded to Gil. "If you'll continue—"

Gil hammered home each point from the brief he had desperately assembled. All too soon, it seemed to him, he reached his summation. "I submit, Your Honor, that in waiting this long to ask for the return of her child, Jeanette Davis has forfeited her rights as a mother; that in failing to apply for custody of Margaret long since, when she was well able to make a home for her and provide for her, she has demonstrated a complete lack of any normal motherly concern for her offspring. In trying now, after twelve years, to get her back, she displays such an utter lack of understanding of her child as a person, or of herself in the role of mother, that I say she is unfit to be this child's mother."

Judge Clement Owsler looked inquiringly at Jeanette. "Well, Mrs. Davis?"

Roger Belden leaned forward to speak, but the Judge forestalled him. "No, Mr. Belden. I want to hear what Mrs. Davis has to say."

Jeanette shifted in her chair and lifted her head just a bit, with an effect not unlike that of a ship figurehead facing into the wind. Her hands lay open in her lap, palms up, as though in appeal.

"I have always wanted to have my child back. For a long time I could do nothing about it because of my parents-in-law; in particular, my father-in-law. Scandal of any kind was anathema to him. If he had ever found out that the girl married to his son had borne an illegitimate child, I—I believe he'd have had me tarred and feathered. I'd certainly have been hustled right out of the family, under—believe me —extremely unpleasant circumstances. Joel would have been made to suffer too; his father would have held him responsible for such a disgrace befalling the family." She glanced at her husband with a look whose tenderness even Gil could have sworn was quite real.

"I love my husband. So I said nothing. Then Joel's mother died, and his father soon after. Still I did nothing about getting Margaret back. I was afraid to. My husband is a very proud man, Judge Owsler. I believed that the discovery of my past, and the lies I'd told to cover it up, would turn him against me. I was afraid he'd feel that I'd betrayed him."

Joel Davis, beside her, reached out and took her hand.

"Yes, I understand." The Judge had taken off the pair of half-glasses. He fiddled with them now, as though the way they were put together might have something to do with the problem before him. "Yet you evidently did tell your husband, finally. What caused you to make that decision?"

Deliberately Jeanette collected the eyes of those present in the room. "Mother love," she said, staring defiantly at the Judge as though daring him to try to attack that. "There can come a time when love of one's child outweighs everything. For me, it came when Enid Weir was murdered. My Margaret with no mother to look after her. And the circumstances of Enid's death . . ." She looked across at Gil, her timing making of the words an accusation.

Deftly Roger Belden picked up the thread of his client's discourse. "What Mrs. Davis is trying to say is that she's genuinely worried about Margaret's safety. With a murder having been committed in the Weir home, and the murderer still unapprehended . . . Your Honor, I've been talking to your Prosecutor, Bill Martin, about the murder of Mrs. Weir. Now I'm well aware that this hearing is not a trial, and that it is concerned with custody, not a killing. But these two matters cannot be separated. In considering my client's application for custody you cannot rule out, when you weigh Gilman Weir's claims, the possibility that he may eventually be charged with the murder of his wife. That he may, in fact, have killed her."

Judge Owsler, after his years on the bench, was clearly not startled or taken aback by this pronouncement. He had no doubt foreseen when he had first heard of the custody matter that the murder would make up part of the case.

He nodded. "I'm aware of the facts concerning Mrs. Weir's demise," he said crisply. "This is a simple hearing, Mr. Belden; there's no jury. So we don't need any dramatics. Gilman Weir, the child's foster father, is not on trial. And since no charge has been made against him, speculation on the subject is out of place here. Let's stick to known facts, if you please. You say now, Mrs. Davis, that you made no move to claim your daughter, nor any revelation to your husband that you had given birth to a child, until after the death of Enid Weir. That's correct?"

"Yes."

"You did not at any time approach Enid Weir to discuss with her the possibility of getting back your little girl?"

"No."

"Have you had any contact with your daughter, or with Enid Weir or with Gil Weir since you gave them your child to raise?"

Jeanette shook her head. "Gil and I agreed I should never come near Margaret, because it would make things unbearably hard for me, and because she—she might guess, somehow. And I've had no contact with Gil or Enid from the day they took Margaret from the hospital in Minneapolis until today. Except that I sent flowers to the funeral. This—this matter of the custody has been handled altogether by Mr. Belden."

"I see. Now, about the home to which you propose to

transfer the child—Mr. Davis, may I ask what your feelings are toward this child of your wife's?"

Joel Davis squared his footfall-player shoulders. "Oh, I want her very much." With his fingers laced together and resting between his knees, he looked across earnestly at Judge Owsler. "For Jeanette's sake, and for mine too. We've wanted children for a long time, but Jeanette's been unable to have another. When she told me, finally, about Margaret—well, there was no doubt in my mind, she *belonged* with us."

"You have no feeling of resentment that this is another man's child? Resentment against your wife or against the child herself?"

"No. No, Your Honor. It's too late for that." There was something a little painful, perhaps self-deriding, about the suggestion of a smile. "It was over with long ago—the engagement to someone else, and the baby; before we'd ever met. The fact that there is a child and that she belongs to my wife—it's like a windfall."

"Um." The Judge sucked in his lips, and thought. "And what did you think, Mr. Davis, about the medical opinions that were given us by two highly qualified physicians?"

Joel Davis frowned. "Well, of course there's something in what they say. But she'll adjust. I'm sure of it. And we'll do everything for her. Everything."

Jeanette leaned forward; in her dark blue eyes was a glowing fervor. "When she's my own child, that link is bound to mean something to her: it has to."

"You're optimistic, Mrs. Davis. I can't blame you for that. But let me ask you: are you prepared to have Margaret fight you tooth and nail? That may happen, you know."

She glanced at Joel, in appeal. "I'm sure that will pass."

"Well, we'll see. I'm going to send for the young lady in a minute or two. Before she joins us, is there anything else—"

"Your Honor," said Belden. "If I may ask a few questions of Dr. Gorse, since he is still with us—"

"Yes, of course."

His questioning was skillful: no references to possible murder charges, but question after question about the effect on a child of the death of the mother, of living under conditions where violence has occurred and might occur again, and the unsettling effect of living five days of the week in someone else's home—as Margaret was doing, farmed out at the home of her foster mother's sister (no relative at all, and a woman already busy with her own four children and a job).

Dr. Milton Gorse looked somewhat embarrassed; after all it was on Gil's behalf that he had made an appearance. "I would like to make clear, however, Mr. Belden, that the personal stress this child is undergoing following the death of a parent and the temporary disruption of her home is not to be compared with the breaking of all old ties, the replacing of everything familiar with things and people that are unfamiliar. I repeat what I said earlier: I strongly advise against transplanting this child into an alien environment. She is not a puppy or a kitten to be moved at will." He glanced at his watch.

"If I may go now, Your Honor . . ."

Dr. Gorse took his departure.

"Your Honor"—Roger Belden had the look of a man of the cloth about to launch into a funeral oration—"we have heard Dr. Gorse's expert testimony as to the shock, the trauma, this child has undergone, and the state of uncertainty and apprehension in which she is now existing. Her foster mother murdered. The crime unsolved. The doctor's last remark I suggest should be disregarded as purely a sentimental plea on behalf of Gilman Weir. Of course this little girl is not a puppy or a kitten! The S.P.C.A. is not the agency in charge of her! Instead, she comes under the Standard Juvenile Court Act, as a child whose environment is injurious to her welfare . . ."

All of them were present now, in the little room.

"Now, Maggie."

She looked up at Judge Owsler.

"You know that this lady sitting on the other side of the room is your real mother?"

"Yes, I know," she said without looking at the lady. She leaned against Gil.

"How do you know this?"

"My father told me. But I don't *want* her to be my mother. I'm *adopted*."

Her mother leaned forward, intent. "Margaret—Maggie?"

Maggie returned her gaze with one of stubborn antagonism. "I remember you," she said accusingly. "I saw you before."

Gil stared down at his daughter—astonished. This was something he hadn't known.

"You mean, Maggie," said Clem Owsler carefully, "that you remember seeing Mrs. Davis before?"

Very slowly she nodded.

"When was this?"

"Ooo-ohhh," Jeanette's child said on a rising inflection, "I guess it was before Halloween sometime, because I was out in the yard collecting the best-colored leaves for my collection—red ones and yellow ones. You dip them in melted paraffin and then press them between wax paper and they stay that way."

"And Mrs. Davis was there?"

"Yes. I noticed she was standing on the sidewalk watching me, and then she came closer and asked who lived there and I told her. She said she guessed she had the wrong address, and she left then and went on down the sidewalk and crossed the street."

The Judge turned to Jeanette. "Is that the way it was?"

"Yes." Her voice was very low. "I just wanted to see what she looked like." She stole a glance at her husband. Joel Davis was clearly taken aback; this revelation was news to him. He chewed worriedly on his lower lip and looked across at Roger Belden in the expectation that he would do something. But Belden could only stare contemptuously at the client who had failed to tell him everything she should have.

"And when was it that this occurred?" Judge Owsler continued.

"About the middle of October, I suppose."

"You still maintain, Mrs. Davis, that you never thought of trying to reclaim your daughter until after Enid Weir was killed?"

Jeanette's eyes flashed. "I didn't say I never *thought* of it. I said I did nothing *about* it until after she was dead."

"That's quite true, Your Honor," Belden stated. "It was not until after Mrs. Weir's death that Joel Davis asked me to undertake the custody matter for him and his wife. In fact it was the news that the first suspect, the man arrested in Chicago, was not the killer that brought Mrs. Davis to the point of telling her husband about the child. It was then that she began seriously to worry about Margaret's—safety." He shot a quick, gleaming look at the Judge, pleased to have gotten in a sideswipe at Gil.

"Ah," said the Judge. "Yet Mrs. Davis did conceal the fact that she had come to Selkirk in October to have a look at her daughter; how am I to be sure other things are not being concealed in—"

"No, Judge Owsler. I swear!" Jeanette protested. "I kept back the fact that I'd seen her simply as a matter of caution. Because I didn't want anyone leaping to the conclusion that—"

Her attorney broke in. "Mrs. Davis was ill-advised, Your Honor, in not telling me of this one fact. I'm sure she feared that suspicion might attach to her, when in fact there is no basis for any such suspicion."

"No basis?" said Gil. "There's no basis either for your implication that I might have killed my wife. There's just as good reason for supposing that it was Jeanette Davis who came to my home, the day—"

"My client could not have killed your wife, if that's what you're getting at. I checked into the matter myself in order to forestall any wild guesses on anyone's part. Mrs. Davis was at her hairdresser's in Indianapolis the afternoon your wife was killed. I can get a sworn statement to that effect if you'd like, or if you'd rather the police checked—"

"They may want to, yes," Gil said. "The name of the place?"

"The—" Roger Belden unzipped his briefcase, but before he could find what he was looking for, Jeanette, searching with trembling fingers through her handbag, produced a small pink card.

"This is the place." Her voice was almost a whisper. Her eyes were on her daughter Maggie, as she leaned nearer to give the little printed oblong to Gil, but Maggie stared straight in front of her without a quiver of interest in her mother.

Belden rezipped his briefcase. "And Joel Davis, of course, is beyond any possible suspicion, Your Honor. In view of the fact, which I believe has been well established, that he knew nothing of the existence of his wife's child until after the murder of Enid Weir, it seems hardly necessary to add that Mr. Davis was miles from Selkirk that afternoon, attending a business meeting. A check with the Harding-Borsay Company—"

Covering all contingencies, wasn't he, thought Gil. He had made sure of Jeanette's alibi, just as he had of her husband's—routinely, whether needed or not. No slip-ups for old Roger Belden.

Gil listened while Joel Davis gave his account of Jeanette's telling him, at last, about her illegitimate child. Not surprising, really, he was thinking, that Jeanette had come anonymously to Selkirk. Given his cousin's female nature, and her undoubted tendency to want to have her cake and eat it too, it would have been more surprising, he realized, if she hadn't come at some time or another, irresistibly drawn to the child that was hers. Just for a look. Did that make her a murderess?

"We wanted her, of course," Joel Davis finished. "So I turned over to Mr. Belden the matter of obtaining custody for us."

"Yes. Um. Thank you, Mr. Davis." Judge Owsler straightened, behind his desk. "I'd like, now, to talk privately with Maggie. If you will all wait in the corridor . . ."

They filed out, to wait in two hostile parties by the Tax Assessor's office. Roger Belden conferred in a low tone with the Davises while Gil stood with Phyll Strothers, both of them frowning, hardly a picture of family solidarity. For all Gil knew, his sister-in-law might heartily approve, even, of Maggie's being given back to the mother she had never known. Such a position would fit in with many of the views she held; poor Jeanette Weir, a victim, thirteen years ago, of the double standard . . .

At last the door to Judge Owsler's sanctum was opened by the Judge himself. "I'm ready for you . . ."

With a miserable, tight feeling in his chest, Gil went in. All the meaning, every bit of good and of happiness that had existed in twenty years of marriage seemed to be embodied in the daughter who had come to be his and Enid's. The void that would be left if she were taken away was something he couldn't begin to imagine.

He took a seat—though not by Maggie, who sat, head bent, behind the Judge's desk, in a chair he had pulled up for her. Gil knew the verdict then, he guessed, just by looking at her—tensed, her eyes cast down. But he hoped he was wrong.

Judge Owsler began. "People expect to get justice in the courts. They expect the fair thing to be done. But Mr. Belden knows, and I hope Mr. Weir remembers, that the purpose of the courts is first and foremost—and last and always, I suppose—to administer the law."

Oh, God, thought Gil. I've lost her.

Maggie was to go at first only on a visit. Friday, Saturday, and Sunday; it being a long weekend because of Thanksgiving.

"Sunday afternoon or evening," Judge Owsler specified, "she's to be returned to her home in Selkirk, so that she'll be ready to attend school on Monday. Her classes at the junior high school here are not to be disrupted; enough else will be, as it is."

"But when she comes with us she'll be going to *private* school," Jeanette interposed. "She needn't continue here in public school."

"I think it would be best for a while, Mrs. Davis. As I told you, any decision made at this hearing is strictly temporary, and subject to review. I have made no final decision on this case."

"But she's my—" Before Jeanette could finish her objection, Roger Belden had gripped her by the arm in a manner that precluded her saying more.

"And the following weekend also?" Belden asked of the Judge. "Maggie is to spend that as well with her mother?"

Judge Owsler nodded. "We'll see, after that, how things are going."

Maggie ate Thanksgiving dinner at Trina's.

"Well, if she'd rather," Phyllis had said to Gil. "I'd supposed you and Maggie would have Thanksgiving dinner with us."

"Thanks, don't count me in either, Phyll. Too much of a family holiday, I'd rather skip it."

"Well—if that's the way you feel." He thought she looked relieved, actually. "Marilyn's home from I.U., of course, so there'll be all the kids. And Sid's coming."

"Sid?"

"Sid Strait. He's a bachelor, you know, no place to go, so I thought we'd invite him."

"I didn't know he was a friend of yours." He'd hardly thought of Sidney Strait since the day of the library-wing dedication, when the new librarian had put his foot into it with Enid. An offense Gil would have expected to find still rankling in the midst of Phyll's carefully collected store of grievances; apparently not?

"Why, yes," Phyll said. "He's a really fine person when you get to know him. Very sensitive. That misunderstanding with Enid, you know, was not his fault . . ."

And so Gil dined alone at home on Thanksgiving, on scrambled eggs.

Early in the evening he drove over to pick up Maggie.

It was Cinny who opened the door of the big old brown-stained shingle house. "Come say hello to Aunt Lucille." No time, was there, for privacy. Shrieks of laughter from above told him the two girls were somewhere upstairs.

It had been years since he'd seen Miss Lucille Howland. She had aged, he saw as he entered the musty, heavily furnished living room; had shrunk and grown wispy; the long, homely face was only fleetingly reminiscent of an earlier Miss Howland—and, too, of her nephew Ted.

"So nice to see you, Gil." The voice—still crisp and authoritative—had not changed; and Gil could almost believe his eyes deceived him—that she had not, after all, grown pitifully old.

"Good evening, Miss Howland."

"I was so sorry about your wife—" Her bright eyes had clouded.

They spoke of Enid; of Maggie and Trina. How different everything was, Miss Howland told him, with Cynthia here —how very lively.

He must talk to Cinny. Must. He signaled her across the

room, and she nodded.

"I must take Maggie home—"

And then he and Cinny stood alone in the huge, anachronistic hall with its dark paneling and the big double stairway to the floors above.

"I was sorry to be so formal on the phone last night," he said. He had called, of course, to tell her the outcome of the custody business. "Afraid to say much for fear my phone's been tapped—or yours."

"Your *phone*—?"

"Having spent some time in the company of Jeanette's lawyer, Roger Belden, at the hearing, I'd say he's not likely to miss any bet that might pay off. If he *is* employing a detective agency—"

"You think so?"

"I don't know. Nothing came up at the hearing to indicate it. Still . . . *someone* certainly must have followed us Saturday night in Kokomo. Could be someone Belden put on my tail, hoping to come up with something damaging—something to use in negotiating with me out of court if there's any snag in his gaining custody of Maggie for Jeanette."

"But surely he wouldn't have given his ace in the hole to anyone else to use—even the Selkirk police. Would he?"

"He might have. He might play it both ways—get me convicted of murder, he hopes, and out of Jeanette's way, or if that doesn't work, use a little personal blackmail with the same result. It would never occur to him that Selkirk's detective lieutenant might tip me off to the Prosecution's case against me—what there is of it—by telling me how much he knew. Not kosher, certainly. But then Orin had his reasons." He kissed her and said regretfully, "Damn it, I've got to be going."

From the foot of the stairs he called Maggie—remembering once again that tomorrow she would be going away. To Indianapolis. To her mother's.

"Incredible," Cinny said very low, as though she had read

his thoughts. "To think she can be taken away from you, just like that!"

"Yes," said Gil.

He drove the two of them home, feeling that this might be the last sane, ordinary evening in the world.

Whatever happened, he must see that Cinny wasn't hurt. But Maggie? There was nothing he could do, was there, to protect Maggie from what was to come.

Chapter 10

It was on Friday that the gun was found. Two boys playing around a bridge south of Selkirk on Route 31, the highway linking Indianapolis and Kokomo, found it in some bushes at the edge of the creek. Whoever had thrown it from the bridge had missed the water, and the sleek black metal shape had lain hidden in a nest of leaves and twigs, in the shelter of the span above.

No fingerprints on it, of course.

But it was Gil Weir's revolver. No doubt of it, with the serial number. And when Orin Hogg—with the sheriff looking on—had test-fired it and back at Headquarters had compared the test-fired bullet with the one that had been removed from the brain of Enid Weir, they knew positively that at last they had the murder weapon.

Orin Hogg secured a warrant for Gil's arrest.

Then he got into his car and drove over, personally, to Gil's house to bring him in.

The Davises, early that morning, had come for Maggie. In a big black Lincoln Continental driven by Mr. Davis.

Maggie had hated the ride down to Indianapolis. Mrs. Davis talked to her as if she were about nine years old. And either her vocabulary was really limited or she didn't think a girl of twelve would understand long words. She kept explaining things, too, that Maggie had known all about for years—as though she'd been born marooned on a desert island and didn't know what the rest of the world was like. Mr. Davis was the one who didn't know anything about children, she said—hesitating over the word "children" as though maybe it was a label she oughtn't to apply, like calling somebody a Jew or a Wop . . .

Well, Mr. Davis certainly hadn't said much; probably he didn't know anything about kids. But neither did his wife.

"And you can't go on calling me Mrs. Davis, you know," Mrs. Davis said to her helpless captive. "How about just using my first name, for now. Jeanette."

The house was beautiful. Maggie would have loved to visit it under other circumstances . . . And be visiting somebody else, too, not the Davises. There was a circular staircase like something out of the movies, going up out of the front hall, and a crystal chandelier as big as a merry-go-round. The kind of floor she'd seen in museums: wood laid out in squares all over. "That's parquet," Jeanette said when she saw her looking at it. And that was something she *hadn't* known, actually.

The living room was all white. Just the place to come in with muddy boots and put your feet up while you watched television—and eat chocolate candy that wasn't M&M's.

"And this is Ruby."

Maggie turned, and there was a colored maid in uniform.

"Hello," she said to Ruby, warming to her on sight as she never could have to Mr. and Mrs. Davis.

It was Ruby, later, who showed her how to work the intercom in her room. Again, it would only have been fun if there were someone she wanted to call on it. As it was, the thing gave her the uneasy feeling of being unable to escape from her unwanted mother; wherever Jeanette might be in the house, Margaret Weir was practically at her fingertips.

"This the blue guest room," Ruby told her. Indeed it was. Pale blue carpet, blue flowered drapes, quilted blue spreads on the twin beds. Even a blue telephone on the table between the beds.

"You don't like bein' here much, do you," Ruby volunteered.

"No."

There was understanding in the large, liquid brown eyes. She smiled. "Neither do I. I got to be some*place,* though. So do you."

"Not here." Maggie's eyes went slowly over the appointments of the room. Not her kind of room at all. "She's supposed to be my mother. But she's not. My mother's dead."

"Yes, I read 'bout that. I'm sorry."

She had one friend here in Indianapolis, anyway. Ruby.

When they'd gone, Gil wandered back into the house.

"What do I call them?" Maggie had asked—seeming, with the question, to have put into a nutshell all that was wrong.

"You'll work something out, I suppose," he'd said.

Couldn't stand it here in the house, he decided. Might as well go downtown to his office, holiday weekend notwithstanding.

He did, and worked for a while, put some stuff on the dictating machine for Barbara, and slowly ground to a halt, unable to bring his mind to focus any longer on legal matters other than his own.

Wearily he stuffed a few items into his briefcase, turned off the lights—it was a very gray day, dark—and locked up. In the parking lot he got into his car and for a minute or two just sat there, gazing into a maze of speculations as gloomy as the weather. Unable to decide what to do, where to go. He switched on the engine and sat a little longer, with the motor warming up the heater, and the radio supplying companionship of a sort.

He had nowhere to go. Couldn't go to Cinny's, that wouldn't do at all until other matters had been cleared up. God, he'd like to just sit and yak to somebody. Somebody he could relax with.

Fred Towse. Why not?

He decided. And started off. Turned out of the parking

lot and headed for the highway south . . . A little way out of town he passed the sheriff's car—always recognizable, with his title emblazoned on the door—going the other way, toward town. Behind him, O.H.—in *his* car. Working on what? he wondered. Oh, well, there were other cases besides the Weir murder.

Though it was as well if Orin hadn't seen him; technically, he wasn't supposed to leave town.

Gil slowed. Some sort of happening up ahead, where the highway crossed a stream: cars parked on the shoulder of the road, and a knot of people down by the water . . . Nothing to see, he concluded; people talking, hands on hips. Whatever had gone on was over.

He picked up speed again. The squared-off fields, brown and empty with winter coming on, flew by. The McCutcheon farm to his right, and he thought of the day that had changed everything so.

He turned west on 32, toward Lebanon. And at Lebanon, south on 39.

And it was then that he got the news on the radio, breaking into it midway as he switched stations. "*—of the murder weapon from a stream near Selkirk. Chief of Police J. D. Blackburn stated that an arrest is expected momentarily.*"

Ah. The tableau by the bridge became suddenly clear—especially when he connected it to the two official cars he'd met, which had obviously just left the scene.

They'd found it. *His* gun, of course; why else would it be missing? And then his scalp prickled. A stream not half a mile from McCutcheons' farm. A bridge he'd passed over the afternoon of Enid's death, on his way to see old Mrs. McCutcheon. Had he just missed the person who'd thrown his revolver over, that day? Or had it been placed there since, by someone who knew where Gil Weir had gone right after his wife had been killed?

They had lunch in what Jeanette called the terrace room. "It used to be an outdoor patio," Mr. Davis explained;

almost his first unsolicited remark. "When I was a boy."

"It's nice." For some reason Maggie felt sorry for Mr. Davis. Maybe because he seemed to be as ill-at-ease as she was. She hadn't thought adults ever were. It must be, like Jeanette said, he didn't know anything about kids; he didn't know what to do about her.

Lunch was delicious. Chicken potpie, jello salad, and custard with sauce. Ruby served it, and they ate at a glass-topped table and there were fingerbowls.

Mr. Davis—Joel, that is; she was to call him that—went someplace after lunch. She saw him go down the driveway in a yellow Stingray. She knew what kind it was because she'd always wanted one.

And after that Jeanette took her downtown. "We'll do some shopping for you," she promised as Maggie, regretting the departed Stingray, seatbelted herself instead into the long black car parked in the circle at the front door.

"Only first I have to get my hair done. A bore for you, I'm afraid, but you see I have a standing appointment on Fridays."

Perversely Maggie pictured an appointment to stand.

"Wouldn't you like to have your hair done too? Styled or—"

A horrid idea. "No. It's all right."

"Your hair curls like that naturally, doesn't it, Maggie? Mine always did."

And for the first time it came home to Maggie that this woman really was her mother. They had hair alike.

But she didn't like her. In fact her sudden recognition of the blood tie as real made Maggie the more determined to fight against it. It was as though the battle were joined, now —a real battle, not play-acting, not courtroom drama on T.V.

She would *not* be Jeanette's child.

She remembered the effect at the hearing when she announced that she had seen Jeanette before. And she remembered the lawyer, Mr. Belden, smoothly, surely, giving the Judge the reason why Mrs. Davis could not have been in Selkirk at the time Mom was killed. She'd been at the hairdresser's.

What if . . .

There was plenty of time, while she waited for Jeanette. Maggie loitered about the front of the beauty shop, leafing through magazines; listening and noticing. The counter where the cash register, the phone and the appointment book were housed was unmanned (unwomaned?), but not five feet away sat a customer, waiting.

The phone rang, and one of the operators, a tired-looking silvery blonde, came from the back of the shop to answer it. Someone making an appointment.

A lady paid for her stiff, meticulously done hair and left.

Phone rang again, and was answered by a plump brunette; someone changing an appointment. The operator was writing in the name, then reversing the pencil to erase the old appointment. She hung up, smiled at the waiting customer— the one that was keeping Maggie from her detective work. "Ready for you now," and Maggie was left alone.

She turned quickly back, in the wide, lined and columned pages of the appointment book, to the date she wanted. Tuesday. The right one. Heart thumping, she scanned the afternoon hours. Even her finger throbbed, with a quickened pulse, as she ran it, searching, over the page. *There!*

Yes, there. Sure enough. In one of the three o'clock spaces, *Mrs. Davis* was written in.

But the impression of another name—a longer name— still showed beneath the penciled script.

Suddenly a white-uniformed figure materialized at her elbow. "Oh." A sharp voice; surprised. "Can I help you . . . ?"

Maggie felt the bottom of her stomach fall out. "I—was looking for the phone book."

"In the drawer." It was the tired-looking silvery blonde. Eyeing Maggie skeptically, she pulled open a drawer and took out the thick Indianapolis book—so much fatter than the Selkirk one. "You want to use the phone?"

"No. I just wanted to look up something."

She waited, still, for Jeanette. And as she sat, legs twined intricately around the lower portions of an aluminum chair, part of a muted conversation drifted out to her from behind some drawn curtains. ". . . trying to get the cash drawer open. I'm sure she was . . . little sneak."

Tears burned behind Maggie's lids. She wished she were home. Home in Selkirk.

She stared, unseeing, at a fat lady stuffed beneath a drier halfway back in the shop. (Her stockings were wrinkled.) . . . Someone's appointment for three o'clock Tuesday— *the* fatal Tuesday—had been erased. Had her mother Jeanette wanted to come in on that day instead of Friday, that week? And she had changed her standing appointment and taken a cancellation?

Or had two names been switched later, for safety's sake, so that Jeanette Davis could point out—if the question came up—that she had been in Indianapolis at that particular time, on that particular afternoon . . .

An arrest is expected momentarily.

That could only be his. And it had not been his old classmate and buddy, Oinky Hogg, who had issued the statement. No. It had been O.H.'s boss, the Chief of Police. The revolver would have been the last bit of evidence they felt they must have before actually charging him and locking him up.

He began to feel terribly conspicuous, out there on the highway. Flat fields stretching away on all sides; oh, a few little undulations here and there, but no place to hide. A great dearth, even, of lanes or crossroads to which he might resort in case of pursuit. Because by now every State Trooper in the area could well be on the lookout for him.

Turn himself in?

No. As a lawyer he knew well enough that the only course to take was to surrender to the authorities, get a good criminal lawyer for his defense, and count on the American judicial system to find an innocent man not guilty. But as an actual fugitive from the law—a man who could all but hear the cell door clanging shut behind him—he could not bring himself to surrender. Not now.

Because . . . well, just how innocent was he? Guilty of loving another woman while his wife was still alive. Womanizer, Orin had called him. The fiction of Barbara and the fact of Cynthia Howland would convict him before the Prosecutor's summation was even reached. Guilt was not relative, it was absolute, in a case like this one.

The determining factor, though, was Cinny. He could not allow the motel business to be presented in court.

And so he must not, as things stood now, get caught.

He'd better call Fred. See if he was there. What he needed immediately was help.

As soon as you want a phone, there isn't one. He started looking. Drove on, drove on. No filling station, no crossroads store, no place with a phone booth. Compulsively he watched the rearview mirror. Not much traffic today; middle of the holiday weekend, hardly anyone going anyplace, it seemed. Except him. All alone on the road—or almost; a wanted man.

Finally. A filling station up ahead. He slowed. Then gunned the motor as it registered suddenly, like an alarm bell in his head, that the vehicle parked beside the building was a State Police car. He sped on by. Kept going.

Nothing but fields. He thought of going into a farmhouse, saying his car had broken down, could he come in and make a telephone call. No. Didn't want to get involved with people. Or trapped in a farm lane.

MA'S PLACE, a sign proclaimed. *Beer, Steak, Chicken in a Basket, Sandwiches. OPEN*. Room back of the building to pull in.

He parked, searched out Fred's number from the stuff in his briefcase, went inside. Pay phone on the wall.

Dialed. Thank God, an answer.

Eyes trained on the road outside the window, as he talked to Fred. A thrill down the spine as a State Police car went by, headed toward Danville. Same one he'd seen?

Out to the car again. (Would the teen-aged, rabbit-toothed counter girl remember him? Identify him for the cops?)

Six more miles and he was threading his way through the back streets of Danville, as instructed. Glad he'd called. Wouldn't have known where Fred's place was. Might have blundered onto the main drag, with police and all.

Oh-oh. Street blocked ahead. Totally. Cars stopped. Clots of people. A policeman leaning into the window of a car standing in the middle of the intersection. Momentary panic. Were they stopping everyone? But how could they know—

And then he saw that it was a wedding. Church. Bride and groom.

Ten minutes later, after a harrowing passage through unknown territory—he'd had to back up, at the church, and had lost his way—he turned into the drive of a big old turreted Victorian house, stashed his car in the open garage as instructed, pried his fingers loose from the steering wheel, got out, closed the garage door, and crossed the drive to the little cement walk leading to a new wing that had been added to the main part of the house.

Fred held the side door open for him. "Well. My friend the attorney—on the lam? I don't believe it!"

"Shut up." But he grinned in relief to be safe somewhere, even temporarily.

Inside, a sitting room with a long bank of windows, hanging ferns, a mirror-back sofa, rocking chairs with antimacassars, needlepoint sidechairs. "Your new taste in decorating?" Gil asked.

"Dig the sewing table." Fred opened the side of a small

piece inlaid with mother-of-pearl, to reveal a choice of scotch, bourbon, or gin, and an assortment of glasses. "What'll you have? You need one, I'm sure. No ice, I have to go out for that."

"Whatever you're having."

"O.K., scotch." He poured two drinks. "This was the apartment my landlord built on for his aged mother, who passed away last year at ninety-eight. And I'm lucky to have this place. Gil, sit down. You'll wear out the rug."

"Ever been a fugitive from justice? Maybe when I get used to it—"

"Just how bad are things?"

Gil told him, leaving out only the motel incident; including the gossip about Cinny, the speculation that had linked them even before Enid's death. "And of course it's true, I'm in love with her. If and when this murder thing is cleared up, we'll be married."

"Best of luck, and congratulations. I always liked Cinny. But if the murder doesn't get cleared up. What then? Flee to South America and live under an assumed name or something?"

Gil stared down at his scotch, finished it off and poured himself another. "I can't believe the thing won't be solved. And soon."

"You think you know who it was?"

"No. But I have a very limited number of possibilities in mind. It's got to be one of them. What I need is a car. Can't use mine—by now the license number's probably been broadcast on an all-points bulletin."

"You're going to do your own sleuthing?" Fred's clean-cut, All-American face broke into a small-boy grin of excitement. "You can have my car, it goes without saying. Unless it's not safe? Old Oinky Hogg might think of me, I suppose, as a logical person to give aid and shelter to some such criminal type as yourself."

"Afraid so."

"Patty's car."

"Oh, I couldn't—"

"Yes, you could. You know you're the only Selkirk friend who hasn't crossed me off their list? Patty appreciates that as much as I do." He reached for the phone. "We outcasts stick together." He winked.

Gil didn't realize until he met Patty how extensively his expectations of her had been colored, first by Enid's views on homewreckers as a class, and second by Enid's highly derivative opinion of Patty in particular, thirdhand through Beth who had never met her either. He had pictured some hard-eyed, opportunistic little roundheels wearing cheap perfume.

Patty wasn't like that. She wasn't pretty; instead, she had style and intelligence. She seemed to Gil to be extraordinarily aware—of herself, without being conceited; of him as a good friend; most of all of Fred, as if he were the sun shining on her.

"Hello." Carefully she set down two brown paper bags, and shook hands. "I'm sorry you have troubles." Dark hair, thin face, too much jaw, long-fringed eyelashes.

She had driven up from Terre Haute immediately after Fred had called, she explained as she shed her coat. Had stopped on the way only for supplies.

"From the supermarket delicatessen." She indicated one of the bags reposing on the small drop-leaf table. She hefted the other one, causing it to clank slightly, and set it down again. "This one's a—sort of emergency kit. Flashlight and so forth. Oh—and one panic item." She gave him an odd, hesitant look. "I didn't know whether to put it in or not. When my brother was looking for a job last year—"

Midsentence she stopped, as a knock sounded on the outer door, and the three of them froze.

Wordlessly they looked at one another. Anyone could have arrived unobserved at the door. Neither the driveway—except for the apron by the garage—nor the little walk could be seen from within; the end wall of the apartment was windowless.

"Police?" suggested Fred in a sibilant whisper, confirming Gil's first and only thought concerning the possibilities.

As Fred stepped to the bank of windows overlooking the back yard and peered sideways, Gil consulted Patty. "Any other way out?"

Quick headshake. "Only through the house, and that door's kept locked."

"It's all right," Fred announced. "It's only my landlord." Easing the door open, he spoke with his caller. "Hello, Harry!" Instant joviality, born of guilt. "What can I do for you?"

A high-pitched, farmland voice—one you could call hogs with—said, "Well, could you move one of these cars? I can't get past to put mine away." And Gil could foresee the awkwardness of Harry's discovering in his garage a changeling car, neither his nor his tenant's.

Fred grimaced, over one shoulder, at his trapped guest. "Sorry about that, Harry." Standing carefully in the narrow crack of the door, he turned again to the outside. "Friend of mine dropped in unexpectedly. No place to put her car, with mine parked out there, I guess. Listen, fella'—just leave yours where it is and I'll put it away? No use your waiting around in the cold while we shuffle all of them around."

"Oh, now—"

"No trouble, Harry. My fault anyway. And if you'll unlock the apartment door, I'll just put your keys right inside in the hall."

"If you don't mind, Fred. Mighty white of you. And say —if you'd like some turkey for sandwiches, Mother's got plenty left—"

"What? Oh, thanks."

And the door was closed and Harry was gone.

"Celestial turkey?" asked Patty, sounding a little breathy

with relief. "I thought Mother had passed on."

"He calls his wife 'Mother.' "

And Gil was for a moment taken back; to the occasion—late August, it must have been—of Enid's turning viciously on him, when he'd said, "Now, now, Mother," as he often had when she fretted over Maggie. "Don't call me that!" He'd first begun to realize, then, how thoroughly their life had been poisoned by Sidney Strait's stupidity.

Fred and Patty redeployed the cars, and the landlord's keys were duly returned.

"Well, that's taken care of!" Fred closed and bolted the door to the main house.

"Here. For you." Patty held out her keyring to Gil. "The large one's for the front door. You'd better stay at my house tonight, don't you think? Much safer than here."

Gil looked mutely at Fred Towse. How far did friendship—?

Fred obliged with an earthy leer. "Don't let it bother you for a moment."

"You probably won't need the key," she added. "Either my father or my brother can let you in. They're expecting you."

Suddenly the world seemed a normal place again. Safe. Blessed with friends. "Thanks, Patty. Thanks very much."

Fred was eyeing the delicatessen bag. "What've we got to eat?" And Gil remembered he'd had no lunch.

"Oh, you're as bad as my brother!" she said comfortably.

Patty laid out the stacks of cold cuts, with cheese, and bread, and pickles, and potato salad. Cheesecake for dessert. Fred started coffee on a hotplate.

It was an amazingly lighthearted picnic, under the circumstances.

"What's your master plan?" Fred asked, falling to.

"Go back to Selkirk and sort of feel my way—I think."

Suggestions were put forth; mulled over. Practical and impractical. Sane and insane. How keyed up they all were, Gil noticed . . . Laughter on a hair trigger.

Dusk outside. Patty got up and drew the drapes, with difficulty closing the gap where they met—resorting, finally, to paperclipping them together. And they made their final plans. When Gil left, after dark, the other two would go also. Patty would drive Fred's car to her house, in Terre Haute, and Fred would take Gil's, going by back routes.

"It should be safe in Patty's folks' garage, for now."

"What if you're stopped on the way?" asked Gil. "Some cop—"

"Better me than you. I'll say you lent me the car while you're away on the West Coast? I dropped you at the airport in Indianapolis—*that* should fix 'em for a while."

When they'd finished eating they waited, still, for full darkness, and Gil remembered to fish out of his pocket the new counterproposal, from Beth's lawyer, for a divorce settlement.

Fred looked it over and threw it on the floor. "She wants me to starve, of course," he said morosely.

"But you expected that," Gil reminded him. And added, "I trust it's occurred to you that you may need to get another lawyer—one that's not in hiding or behind bars . . ."

Patty sucked in her cheeks. "Why d'you think we're making all this effort for you? Pure self-interest!"

He liked Patty. Liked her so much better than he ever had liked Beth Towse. Fred's matured taste was better? Or maybe it was like he'd said—Beth had latched onto him in grade school and he'd had no chance to escape her. Not till now. A little girl wanting to play house, and getting her way.

Gil stirred restlessly and plucked at an edge of the drape. Dark enough? He thought so. He stood up.

"Time to go, I think." He shrugged into his overcoat and scooped up the bag of emergency gear Patty had provided.

"Well, good luck," Patty said. "With things in Selkirk."

"Can't thank you enough," he tried lamely. You couldn't really thank people for something like this. "Both of you."

"You'd do the same for me," Fred said. "Except that I'd never be fool enough to get myself in such a fix."

"Don't be too sure," Gil answered darkly.

He went out. Into a hostile world.

Yes, indeed. The search for him was on. The details made the six o'clock news. Sought for the slaying of his wife a little more than three weeks ago. Missing from his home since this morning; he was thought to have fled the state by car.

Gil smiled grimly in the darkness.

He'd be very careful.

He had two suspects on whom to concentrate. For one of them, the motive would have been money; for the other, possession of Maggie.

And he had thought and thought about that lie someone had told O.H.: that he, Gil Weir, had been seen east of Walnut Street, going toward home, not long before Enid had been found shot to death.

Why Walnut Street? Why Walnut instead of Elm Street or Linden, either of which was still closer to Gil's home? The best answer seemed to be that Orin's informant was someone who had had reason to be on Walnut Street at the time. In this connection one name kept popping up in his mind as the logical one. Other reasons, too . . .

There were no roadblocks. Well, they'd be useless, wouldn't they, from the official point of view—this close to Selkirk, when the bird had presumably flown.

Nor was he being tailed—not this evening, not earlier today—by any private detective; if there ever had been one . . .

He came circumspectly into town; this was no time to be picked up for any sort of traffic violation.

Streetlights. They made him uneasy.

Block by block, he made his way to Phyll's house. Cruised by, saw no sign of a stakeout (really, Orin didn't have the men to spare for that), went on around the corner and, cutting his lights, drew in to the curb, near the entrance to the alley that bisected this block of houses. The back way seemed definitely safest.

No sign of anyone around—no cars coming or going, no people on the sidewalk. He got out and, hurrying into the narrow shelter of the alley, walked softly along between the dark garages lining it on either side. Came abreast of Phyll's —a structure nearly as ugly as the Strothers house; looked in. Her car was parked there but Benson's wasn't. Damn. He'd have to come back.

O.K. Next thing was to get in touch with Barbara—he'd already decided that. He turned back and began to retrace his steps.

Safely in the borrowed car again, he drove across town to the old-fashioned square house in which Barbara lived—all alone, since the death of her father. Everything looked quiet, but he drove around the block twice to be sure, and then parked on the street behind and cut through a yard and a hedge and some bushes. Making his way from tree to tree, pausing at each in the shelter of its trunk, he reached a lighted window and peered in.

Barbara was alone, luckily, and watching T.V.

He rapped on the glass with a gloved fist.

What happened next might have come straight out of a horror movie: the girl turning, all-unknowing, from happy participation in her program to find herself staring eyeball to eyeball at the Glob, the Thing, the Creature, or whatever, pressing its formless mass against the frail glass only feet away.

Barbara's features froze in a mask of terror. And then she was pushing herself up out of her chair, moving awkwardly as though with muscles half-paralyzed by fright, and, as he shouted her name, trying to stop her, fled the room.

Damn. Barbara's Peeping Tom. He'd forgotten.

She was undoubtedly phoning the police.

He moved to another window, trying to catch sight of her. No luck. Now what—

The sound that reached him from behind was too late; if he had not been concentrating so completely on what was going on inside the house, he might have whirled to meet his attacker, or dodged to one side and then away. As it was, he started to turn, only to find himself grasped from behind.

"*All* right!" a voice said. "Now—" But the sentence was never completed. Gil bent forward and to the right, pulling his captor with him, and then threw himself back and to the left as hard as possible, slamming the unseen assailant, who was fastened to his back, sharply against the side of the house —hopefully catching him on the elbow.

There was a grunt and Gil wrenched himself loose. Made it around the corner of the house and dodged behind the trunk of a large tree. None too soon. He heard the other man coming after; heard him round the house, hestitate, go on a few feet and stop.

Gil edged around the trunk, keeping it between them. The crunch of dry leaves told him exactly where his unknown adversary was. And he did not think this was Barbara's Peeping Tom; the voice, with it's "*All* right!" had had the tone of authority. Police?

He sneaked a look and in the light from the windows of the Dresser house could see the man standing not twenty feet away.

Gil took off his right glove and put it in his pocket. Carefully he bent his knees—hoping they wouldn't crack—till his hand touched the ground; felt around the base of the tree for something to throw. A twig. No good. Leaves. Better watch it or they'd rustle under his fingers. Something round and hard—a walnut? Yes.

He eased back to a standing position; raised his arm, cocked his wrist, and fired the walnut, willing it to go as far as possible toward the street in front. Heard it fall. And so did his unknown stalker, because there was quick movement, going away from him.

Keeping the walnut trunk between them Gil retreated into

the shadows, took refuge behind one of the trees he had used only a few minutes before in his approach. He smiled in the darkness, and the rapid beating of his heart felt good.

The man disappeared around the front of the house. And Gil took to his heels. Made it back to the car. As he started the engine and pulled away from the curb the whine of a siren came to him from the distance. He lowered the window a couple of inches so that he could hear it more clearly. Yes, Barbara had called the police.

Then who had that been in her yard? Not the police?

In any case, he'd better get the hell out of this neighborhood before the patrol car got here. He headed back toward Phyll's, keeping an ear tuned to the sound of the Law rocketing through the night.

He was back again, parked by the alley leading to Phyll's garage. He sat motionless behind the wheel, in simple animal terror.

Not the struggle in Barbara's yard, with his near-capture, that had caused it; no. He had found that actually exhilarating. Nor was it the threat of discovery, here in familiar territory. Nor any other lurking danger that might beset him during the evening. No.

Panic item, Patty had called it. She hadn't realized how truly she had spoken. Gil had reached, in the darkness, into the paper bag—which he had placed on the floor beneath the dashboard; groped in it for the flashlight Patty had told him it contained. And encountered there an unknown, unimaginable furry object.

It had been a moment of pure horror—before reason had told him it couldn't, *couldn't* be alive. (Mice. He'd had a lifelong dread of mice. Rats? Even worse.)

Well, he was recovering now. But slowly. He'd risked the tiny map-light under the dash (queasy about reaching for the flashlight in the bag, until he *knew*), and found that it was not fur, but hair. A wig. Male, blond, crewcut—he'd found on lifting it out; ghoulish-looking without a head inside it.

Her brother's, no doubt. When he'd been looking for a job? Probably one of those long-haired kids. Patty's explanation had never been completed—Fred's landlord had come just then.

His shrieking nerves subsided, finally, but still he sat there, reluctant—very reluctant—to get out of the car. What did he really think he was going to accomplish? A man of forty-four? Skulking around in people's yards? In alleys? Though surely not in a blond wig—no, he refused to go that far. (The thing was back in the bag now, together with the claw hammer and the chisel which were its companions. The flashlight was in his overcoat pocket.)

Well. No use putting it off. He dragged himself out of the comfort and security of Patty's car and made his way again up the alley.

Whereas on his earlier trip along here the darkened garages had seemed to offer shelter and safety, now the yawning blackness of open doors and the secretiveness of half-closed ones suggested, more than anything else, an ambush. He guessed he was becoming a little jumpy, what with one thing and another.

The spot next to Phyllis's car—when he reached his objective—was still empty.

It was a long, freezing wait for Benson. (Was Phyll's eldest son capable, really, of committing a murder? Who knew? Who understood kids today?) To keep the blood circulating in his cold, cold feet, Gil alternately paced the dark little back walk, and took refuge in the garage from the chill wind, sitting inside on the workbench that had been Bee-jay's in the years before he'd taken off for California.

It was while he was pacing the particularly shadowy patch of the walk in which he felt safest that a car pulled up in front of the Strothers house. Quietly Gil slipped past the darkened windows of the family room, ducked under the living-room window which shone yellowly into the night, and flattened himself against the siding behind the downspout at the front corner.

Phyll . . . and Sidney Strait, coming up the walk and conversing in low tones. Then silence, as they reached the front stoop. Gil craned his neck. Selkirk's Women's Lib leader was kissing the town's head librarian. Hmm . . .

She opened the door, then, and they went inside; and Gil retired to the rear of the property to resume his pacing.

He had just gone back into the garage, out of the wind, when light wavered along the alley. He stepped behind Phyll's car.

It was Benson, all right; he pulled into the garage, cut the engine and the lights. And nearly jumped out of his skin when his uncle collared him, there in the dark.

"Benson, listen here—"

"What the—oh, hello, Uncle Gil." And then, "Uncle *Gil?* Jesus, I thought you'd split. At least the police—"

"I want to talk to you, Benson."

"Yeah, sure. Just a minute, I'll turn the light—"

"No. No light. Now, listen . . . What made you think you could tell a lie like that to Lieutenant Hogg and get away with it?"

"A lie? What lie?" He tried unsuccessfully to remove himself from Gil's grip.

"That you saw me during the period of time in which your aunt was killed; going past the Shell station at Walnut, toward home?"

"Me? Huh-uh."

Gil had him blocked—backed into the corner between the workbench and the wall. "Didn't you? According to my figuring, you're the *only* one who would have."

Vigorously Benson shook his head.

"To throw suspicion off yourself."

"No! No—no! Off *myself?*"

"Does Lieutenant Hogg know that you wouldn't have been working at the gas station that day, because Tuesday is your day off? *I* know that, though."

His victim had ceased struggling, and merely gaped at him in horrid fascination.

"There's quite a circumstantial case, Benson, that can be put together to show—for instance, I guess you've probably known for years where I kept my revolver; the number of times you Strothers kids have played hide-and-seek in the bedrooms at my house—well, I'd be very surprised to learn that you haven't been through all the drawers. Add to that the fact that *if* you had my revolver, and had used it, you'd have known exactly where to dispose of it—say that night, or the next day—right where you knew I had been immediately after the murder. Because you were sitting there in the kitchen, the evening of the day Enid was killed, when I told your mother how the State Police had located me out at the McCutcheon farm."

The boy had stopped protesting, and Gil felt him shiver— whether merely with the cold, there was no telling.

"And of all the reasons anyone might have had for killing your aunt, no one had a better one than you. All that money." Yes, indeed; Benson's massive discontent with his lot here in Selkirk, his hatred—wasn't it?—of Marilyn because she was the one who rated tuition money, his lifetime of resentment at the near-poverty to which his father's desertion had doomed him . . .

Gil's eyes had adjusted so thoroughly to the dark that even in the black cavern of the garage he saw the strange, incredulous look that crossed Benson's face; light from the back of the house, filtering weakly through the small panes of the garage's one window, showed the lightness of skin, eyeballs and teeth.

"You mean she did leave me some money?"

Gil frowned. What was the boy talking about? *"Leave* you some money?"

"Well, I hoped she might. A *bequest*—isn't that what they call it? Some sort of bequest. That's why I asked you when the estate would be settled. I didn't want to ask outright if she left me anything in her will, I thought it'd sound greedy."

Gil was silent. Surely Benson wasn't faking ignorance? "Benson . . . you didn't know that all your Aunt Enid's money—that's her half of your Grandmother Kinsey's estate —comes to your mother now, to do whatever she wants with?"

"*All* . . . to my *mother?*" He broke off, almost in a squeak.

"Yes. Your grandmother left it that way. Your Aunt Enid had what they used to call 'female trouble' and finally had a hysterectomy, so she couldn't have any children. Your grandmother's will took that into account. She wanted her two daughters and her *own* grandchildren to have the good of her money—not me, for instance, or an adopted child like Maggie."

Benson sagged against his father's old workbench. "And she never told me! Mom! A part of that garbage she's always giving me about standing on your own two feet, I suppose. She rode me enough about hitting the books as it was, all through school; I suppose she thought I'd never lift a finger if I knew we were going to inherit money." He stared thoughtfully out into the darkness of the alley.

"Well, you wouldn't have inherited—not *yet*—if your Aunt Enid hadn't been murdered—"

"Look, Uncle Gil." Benson seemed to pull himself together. He straightened the hunched shoulders and looked his uncle in the eyes. "I'm sorry. I thought you'd killed Aunt Enid yourself. For her money. Never occurred to me you wouldn't get most of it—"

"Except for a bequest here and there?"

Benson wasn't even listening. "Since you don't get it, though . . . But, see, I thought you shot her and were getting away with it."

"So you've been trying to establish my guilt?"

"Well . . ."

"Was it you, by any chance, who followed me to Kokomo?"

Benson looked startled. "Oh! You knew about that?"

Not some hireling of Roger Belden's, then.

"I really am sorry, Uncle Gil. And believe me, I didn't like telling Lieutenant Hogg—especially on Mrs. Howland's account. But then I thought she oughtn't to go on being mixed up with you, either, if you'd—if you really had— Jesus, I'm sorry!"

"And the lie? About seeing me near home the afternoon of—"

"Oh. Oh, yeah. Well, you see I thought as long as you were guilty it wouldn't hurt to make that up—because you oughtn't to be *allowed* to get away with murder . . ."

"I'm just glad, Benson," Gil murmured, "that you've never even thought of taking up the law when you go on with your schooling. Don't. Don't ever."

"I can see now—obviously, if you thought *I* killed her, you couldn't have."

"Thanks a lot," Gil said dryly. "You sure?"

"Oh, yeah. I'm sure. *Now* I am. But who did kill Aunt Enid?"

"That, Benson, is why I'm out here running around in the dark and waylaying people in garages and so forth. I'm trying to find out. By the way—have you been spying on my secretary?"

"Barbara Dresser? Well, I was. Till I found out she wasn't the one. See, I happened to overhear Mom and Mrs. Towse talking—I wasn't at work that day because of the funeral—"

"You *happened,* by *chance,* to hear—"

"Well—" Benson seemed to squirm a little. "If you're in the upstairs bathroom in our house, and you open the laundry-chute door and stick your head partway down—"

It was a charming mental picture Gil formed of his nephew hanging head downward into the waist-high opening of the laundry chute. (Which Gil happened to remember because he'd once dropped Beejay Strothers down it into the clothes hamper in the basement, when they were boys.) A quite remarkable position.

"It was Mom and Mrs. Towse who said you and Barbara—"

"Yes, I see. Well, Barbara and I didn't *anything,* as a matter of fact. Benson, you weren't over there tonight spying on Barbara?"

"At Barbara's? No. Listen, can I do anything? To help? You sure are in one Christ-awful spot."

"Thanks in good measure to you. Haven't you any redeeming qualities, Benson?"

"Afraid not. Like father, like son, my mother tells me."

"Don't be so glib about it. Your father was a great improvement on you, believe me. Look, though—I need to telephone."

"Come on in."

"Can't. Sidney Strait's in there with your mother."

"Oh. Yeah. Him."

They closed up the garage and went around the house to the front. Strait's car still stood there, parked under the streetlight.

Around to the back again, and they waited, Phyll's son explaining meanwhile the meeting of minds and merging of goals that had apparently taken place (again overheard?) when Sid had sketched out for Phyllis how her cause should be the rights of the individual—not only women but any individual, and certainly single people such as Sid himself, who were not only taxed unfairly, but were discriminated against, often, by prospective employers or landlords.

Benson was stamping his feet to keep them warm. "Hey," he said, growing impatient. "I think it's safe enough. Old Sid'll be in the living room with Mom. She doesn't entertain *him* in the kitchen. Come on in, I'll stand guard . . . And you don't want to run into Mom, either," he added as they felt their way across the frozen grass. "She believes you killed Aunt Enid."

Gil came in, waited till Benson had stationed himself on the other side of the door giving onto the back hall which lay between the kitchen and the front part of the house. And then he called Barbara on the kitchen wallphone. (Business first.)

"Barbara—the police gone? This is your employer inquiring."

"Gil? Oh, my goodness, where are you? You know they've got a warrant for your arrest—"

"Yes, I know that. Barbara, listen. That was me knocking at your window earlier this evening. I wanted to talk to you. But who was the other guy? Somebody in your yard who almost caught me."

"Oh. Oh, that was you? Scared me to death! Why it was Bud Ertz out in the yard. You know him, he's a cop. Lives just up the street from me. He's been watching the house off and on ever since that prowler; you remember—the face at the window? Since Bud lives so close, you know. He was outside calling his dog when he saw a car go very slowly around the corner of my block. He waited and the same car came around again—"

(So much for caution, thought Gil.)

"Naturally he investigated—and found someone—that really was you?—sneaking up to the house."

"He didn't recognize me?"

"I think he only saw you from behind. He guessed, though, that it might be." (Yes, thought Gil, I'm sure he did. And visualized a dragnet tightening, tightening, all around Selkirk.)

A sound from the other end of the kitchen. Gil turned his head. (Jumpy, still.) But there was only the door from the little half-bath, and it was closed. Must've rattled in a draft.

"By the way, Barbara—you can forget about your prowler,

Peeping Tom, or whatever. I think that was my nephew trying to spy on me—and on everybody I know, I guess. He seems to've thought I was a murderer. Now, listen to me, Barbara . . . I am *not* surrendering to the police, so don't tell them I've been here in Selkirk." (Quick glance at the window, black and uninformative. Even now, they could be—) "And tomorrow morning, early, I want you to call Lieutenant Hogg. Ask if he'll do me a large favor and find out whether Jeanette or Joel Davis, either one of them, owns a gray car. They have a black Lincoln, for a starter, but I want to know what else they drive. O.K.?" (Not that there was any more reason than there ever had been to believe in the gray car Maggie claimed to have seen, but when it was just about the only hope left to him . . .)

"But, Gil, I'm sure Lieutenant Hogg won't—"

"We're old friends—or used to be. He just might oblige."

"O.K. If you say so. Anything else?"

"Not right now."

He said good-by, hung up, and dialed Cinny.

Sidney Strait had excused himself to go and wash his hands. Actually he was always washing his hands; whether he had touched anything with them or not, after a certain length of time they inevitably began to feel unclean, as though germs had settled on them out of the air. He told himself it was because of his working with books that he kept them so well scrubbed; it would be horrifying to leave a greasy thumbprint of the flyleaf of one of the volumes entrusted to his care at the library. But it was a habit, by now, and frequent hand washing gave him peace of mind.

He left Phyllis in the living room, stepped into the adjoining family room, which was dark, the children having gone off to bed, and opened the door to the little powder room, where he switched on the light. Scrubbed his hands—Lava soap, how nice (he must remember to get himself some)—inspected his teeth in the mirror for plaque, and found himself listening to part of a conversation on the other side of the door that opened to the kitchen. A male voice.

". . . almost caught me." Just the end of a sentence there, and a silence, as though the speaker were listening. *Caught me?* Gilman Weir. The name leaped to mind immediately, for the very good reason that he and Phyllis had been discussing Gil much of the evening: her brother-in-law's apparent disappearance; her conversation with the police this afternoon; Phyllis's own conviction that he was guilty.

Phyll wasn't hiding him, Sid was sure. The man was in the kitchen without her knowledge. Talking on the phone?

He switched the light off. Quietly he turned the doorknob. Eased the door inward a crack and put one eye to the opening. Yes, Gil Weir. Easy to recognize him even though he scarcely knew the man, having talked to him only the once, at the dedication ceremony; Mr. Weir had been out the day he'd gone to his law office to complain about the trouble Mrs. Weir was making with the library board, trying to get him fired.

There was no doubt, even from this angle, of who it was.

He eased the door shut, and the latch clicked lightly as he let go of the knob. In sudden haste he retreated into the family room, luckily without making a sound. Wouldn't do to be caught eavesdropping—not by someone that much taller and brawnier than he was, and a desperate man besides, someone trying to flee the police.

And that was the answer to the question of what to do about Mr. Gilman Weir: he'd sic the police on him.

He took Phyll with him. In a masterful set of maneuvers he got the two of them into their coats, shushed her up when she started to ask a question, and only when they were safely in the car and moving did he explain.

"Don't worry," Gil said to Cinny, invisible at the other end of some two miles of phone wire. "I just wanted to let you know what I'm trying to do." He'd explained, in the briefest possible way, as much as he could.

"Don't worry? Sure. But thanks for the advice. Darling—you won't get yourself cut down by police bullets, trying to escape . . ."

"No. I won't do *that*."

"Be awfully careful. And—good luck?"

"Till I see you, then." He hung up.

Cinny Howland listened for a moment or two to the heartless, nobody-there emptiness of the dial tone, then set the phone gently back in its cradle.

Till I see you. When would that be? When someone else was discovered to have killed Enid? She could visualize years of letters from far places, reading, *Someday, when my name is cleared and I can come back to the U.S. . . .* Or phone calls in the night, like this one: *No, not too far away. I can't tell you where. I'm on the track of something . . .* Yes, someday. Someday they'd be together, wouldn't they? . . . And she saw herself taking him little gifts in prison, on visiting day. *Yes, darling, another appeal. This time—*

She bit down on a knuckle of her clenched right hand. She mustn't cry. That wouldn't do any good at all. But she loved him so much. Had, all her life; even Ted hadn't changed that fact, happy as she'd been with him. Gil was her first love, and still her love . . .

Helpless anger swept over Gil when he had hung up. There seemed to be nothing he could do to get himself out of this impossible situation. Life, liberty, and the pursuit of happiness—all *verboten*.

He summoned Benson from the hall.

"They're being awfully quiet," his nephew reported. "I didn't look, but I think this thing's getting serious."

"Then congratulations! Maybe you'll have a new father."

Gil left, then, letting himself out the back door. And halfway across the backyard ran right into the arms of the police . . .

"How did you know I was there?" he asked as they sped downtown.

"From Mrs. Strothers, and the fellow runs the library? Mr. Strait. They flagged down our patrol car and told us."

"Oh." The anger was back—with a focus. Sid Strait. And there was something else: he must have noticed it subconsciously, when he'd seen Sid's car, parked under the streetlight. Now he remembered. The car Strait drove was a Dodge, not very new. And it was gray.

Chapter 11

It was morning. Saturday morning. The sheriff was letting Lieutenant Orin Hogg use his office, adjacent to the little block of cells in the Selkirk jail, in which to talk to Gil Weir.

"Believe me, Gil, I've checked into everything I possibly could, trying to find someone besides you to arrest for this murder. Finding your revolver just plain nailed the lid on the case."

"On a very circumstantial case, O.H. God, you know it is."

"Agreed. But still a case. All there."

"You're really satisfied with it, Oinky?" (Orin looked up sharply at the old nickname. Gil had meant him to: reminder of a shared boyhood.) "What about the gray car Maggie saw parked in front of the house? *I* believe it was there. Sidney Strait, by the way—who's responsible for my being caught last night—has a gray Dodge—"

Orin nodded. "I checked up thoroughly on Strait—long since. Asked the police in Maybridge, where he came from, about him. Seems to be O.K. No record of any irregularities, or—"

"I can match him there, so what does that prove! You've got no record on me, either, on the police blotter, my friend.

"Orin—something else, then. Still on the gray car. You weren't in court when my daughter announced out of a clear blue sky that back in October, before Enid was killed, Jeanette Davis had come to the house. To our house. Jeanette was taken aback, let me tell you, and her lawyer too, when Maggie said she'd seen her mother there. Because Maggie had supposedly never laid eyes on my cousin Jeanette, not since we took her as an infant. Belden, the Davises' lawyer, tried to smooth the whole matter over, but—"

"Judge Owsler told me all about it." Orin frowned, and shook his head. "The Judge phoned me after the custody hearing, asked me to check on both the Davises before your daughter actually went to stay with them. In case, you know; with the murder still unsolved—"

"And?"

"I made the calls myself, Gil—Judge wanted 'em checked in a hurry, it being already late afternoon, on Wednesday. Mrs. Davis was at the beauty parlor at the crucial time, and her husband was up in Fort Wayne attending a meeting all afternoon, according to his secretary, who was quite sure of it. So you see . . ." He spread his hands, "And remembering how positive your kid seemed to be about the gray car, I checked with Motor Vehicle Registry. The Davises own two cars. One's a Lincoln Continental—black. Registered in Jeanette Davis's name. The other's a yellow Stingray, in his name. Satisfied?"

"Oh." It was a relief, certainly, to know Maggie was in safe company. Not that he'd really thought Jeanette—

But his eyes strayed to the barred window of the sheriff's office. Who, then? Who?

If there was any longer a way out of all this, Gil couldn't see it. The full meaning of that expression, "up against a blank wall," came clear, and real—and high, and wide, and hard and cold to the touch.

There was a sort of secret smile on Jeanette's face when Maggie came down the circular staircase that morning.

"Come here, darling, I want to talk to you."

How could you call someone darling when you hardly

knew them? Hardening her heart on the way, Maggie trailed into the untouchable-looking white living room after Jeanette.

She was beautiful, her original mother, but that was all Maggie would allow her; she sat down on a long white velvet sofa, and reluctantly Maggie took the other end and settled into place.

"I imagine you'll be staying on here, Maggie. For good. Not going back to Selkirk."

"No," she said hotly. "That's not so! I'm to go home tomorrow. Sunday." But the glint of triumph in the other's brilliant dark-blue eyes told her she was mistaken—it was not to be that way.

"I'm sorry to have to tell you . . ." (She wasn't sorry; Maggie could see that.) "Gil's been arrested for murder."

"He's—" Maggie broke off. *For murder . . . for murder* . . . The words seemed to echo in her mind, hollowly, like something from the soundtrack of a psychological horror movie. For the murder of her mother. Her mother, Enid.

"But he didn't! He didn't kill anyone!"

Cinny felt numb. Today was a continuing bad dream; had been ever since she'd received the initial shock when she'd unfolded the Indianapolis *Star* this morning.

Gil—

With a tight face, she told Trina, when she woke, that Maggie's father had been arrested. For the murder he hadn't committed.

Her own tension must have come through with the news, because Trina asked, "You're pretty upset about it, aren't you, Mom? I mean not just for Maggie." Ted's daughter, with Ted's long face and humorous mouth, but with light hair like Cinny's own, hanging straight and shining to the middle of her back. Still in her pink pajamas, looking up at her mother from the edge of the bed, and asking her to level.

"Yes, I'm extremely upset." She tried to force a brave little smile, and failed. "In fact, I'm clobbered by this happening to Gil."

"Are you and—you and Mr. Weir going to get married? If they let him out of prison again, I mean?"

"Yes—if it's all right with you, that is."

Trina nodded and laid a cheek against her drawn-up knees. "Me and Maggie thought so. He better not have to stay in—"

"Maggie and I," Cinny corrected softly, automatically. So glad that Trina knew. Had known. And Maggie too.

For all the good it would do anyone now . . .

Maggie had fled to her room.

It must be true about her father. Jeanette wouldn't make up a thing like that, because it would soon enough be proved false.

But no matter what, Maggie wasn't going to stay here.

She must be careful, though, not to alert Jeanette to her intentions. So she needed help. She rubbed away some dumb tears.

Ruby? She tried calling the kitchen on the intercom. Then remembered that Ruby wouldn't be there. This week, she'd explained to Maggie, she had Saturday off. No Ruby, then.

As the fact of her isolation sank in, Maggie's new, beautiful, expensive, hated home seemed to grow larger, and lonelier, and even sinister. It was a place she must get out of.

Well. She'd go for a walk. Make a break for it?

But at the bottom of the stairs Jeanette was waiting for her.

"Maggie, you haven't had breakfast."

She was led away to the big white all-tiled kitchen with its acres of counterspace and walls lined with handsome orange-colored cabinets. Jeanette fixed bacon and eggs, and little biscuits. And watched her eat.

"I think I'll go for a walk," Maggie said, heart in mouth, when she had finished.

"Oh, it's too cold! Let's go somewhere in the car—why not? Maybe we'll think of something fun to do."

"If you want to." There was no use to struggle, was there? So that was settled.

Her blood-mother put on a long-haired fleecy coat, cream-colored, and took down Maggie's coat from where it hung in the front closet, and they went out the side door and walked back along the drive past the winterized swimming pool—cheerless, cold-looking, with its cover on. They went on beyond the pool, through a dead rose garden, to the big three-car garage that Maggie hadn't been in. There was an ornamental weathervane, on the roof—a cock. And trellises on the side, with dead vines on them.

No chance, with Jeanette in charge of her, to get away. Maybe later on—

Jeanette opened the side door to the garage; she stepped daintily in, holding the door for her daughter, turning her head with a warm, including glance of the dark blue eyes. Coming in after her, into the penetrating chill of the unheated building, Maggie went around behind the big black Lincoln in order to get into it on the far side. And received a stunning shock.

The yellow Stingray wasn't there; Joel must have gone off in it this morning. But between its empty space and the shiny black Lincoln stood the gray car.

There was not a moment's doubt in her mind. It was the one that had been parked in front of the house the day she and Meegan had walked by it on their way to Girl Scouts. The day her real mother had been killed.

She knew it by the little design sticking up at the front of the hood—a three-spoked circle that looked like a peace sign. Ah. She'd forgotten that, hadn't she, till she saw it, recognized it, now.

With her heart beating uncomfortably fast she opened the door of the black car and got in, so very clearly aware that she was the only one in the world who could help her father.

She alone—besides Jeanette—knew where the gray car had been.

Jeanette was making the garage door go up behind her—though Maggie scarcely noticed. (After all, she knew all about automatic garage-door openers; Lisa's family had had one for years.)

She moistened dry lips and said, "I thought Mr. Davis—Joel—had a *yellow* car."

"He does. A Stingray." Jeanette backed out and started the door on its downward journey.

"Then whose is *that* one?" She pointed just as the closing door cut the last of it from sight.

"The Mercedes? Oh, that's a company car. Joel's company bought it for him to use. We both drive it, actually."

"Oh, I see."

And Maggie was remembering the erasure, where some other name than Davis had been written in the appointment book. Jeanette had not (had she!) been sitting under a hairdrier on that afternoon; instead she had driven the Mercedes to Selkirk, to see Enid Weir.

Jeanette stood, preoccupied, in the kitchen. They'd be three for lunch—Joel had said he'd be back . . .

The drive with Maggie had been a total fiasco.

"It's not *my* fault," Jeanette had said, trying to get to the root of the trouble, "that this has happened and Gil's in jail—"

"Isn't it?" Very uptight, her daughter.

How unreasonable of the child! Just as if—

Coincidence. Coincidences did happen, didn't they? Life was full of them . . . Decide that you want your child back and abracadabra your daughter's foster mother is killed and her foster father jailed for the murder. Coincidence. It would have to be.

Why did she feel so uneasy?

A sound. What was it?

She looked around. From the intercom? And then there was a little ding from the phone on the wall beside it. Maggie was calling someone. Listen in? Because she'd give anything, right now, to know what her daughter was thinking . . . Her fingers curled around the handset, and as she lifted it the two voices—one on the intercom and its echo on the phone—merged into one.

"*Trina, listen.*"

Trina. Her little friend in Selkirk.

"*I'm sure now that Mrs. Davis killed my mother.*"

As she listened, Jeanette's mind became terribly clear, and her body seemed to fill with a cold emptiness that caused a kind of pain. A gray Mercedes, Maggie was saying; parked in front of the Weir house that afternoon . . . Coincidence? It was the first Jeanette had heard of anyone's having seen an unidentified car there that day. It hadn't been mentioned at the hearing. Hadn't been in the papers—not the Indianapolis paper, anyway.

"*No use to tell the police. They wouldn't believe me, because when I told Lieutenant Hogg before, he thought I just made it up.*"

Trembling violently, still holding the phone to her ear, Jeanette sat down. This wasn't possible. Not possible.

She came to with a start. ". . . *Mom'll call the Judge,*" the voice of Maggie's friend was saying. "*And then she'll come for you . . . Mrs. Davis can't keep you prisoner, can she?*"

"*I don't know. I think maybe. But tell your mom to come fast, if she can!*"

Dial tone on the phone.

And the intercom was silent. They'd hung up. She must *do* something. Must cope somehow. The Judge—Judge Owsler—was going to be informed. And the mother of Maggie's friend was—was coming.

She didn't remember going up the stairs, but, like a new scene in a movie, all of a sudden there she was, on the second floor, taking the key out of the keyhole of her own bedroom, going on to Maggie's room, the blue guest room.

She knocked, and then opened Maggie's door. There she sat, her beautiful little daughter, with the dark, dark blue eyes and the dark hair. Weir features, especially the prominent nose and the shaping of the forehead.

"I heard you," she announced harshly. "You left the intercom on." Maggie looked stricken, as her eyes turned to the gadget, the panel on the wall that had betrayed her.

Jeanette's fists were clenched tightly, so that the key she held hurt her fingers. "I don't know how you could think I killed your mother. No matter what your feelings are about me, I'm not that kind of person!"

Did Maggie believe her? There was no telling. Jeanette crossed the room and, leaning over beside the night table, yanked the telephone jack from its socket. She carried the blue phone back with her to the door and set it on the hall floor outside.

"I'm locking you in," she said, "till Joel comes home. I've got to talk to him. We'll decide, then, what to do."

She could hardly see, as she locked Maggie's door from the outside. Tears blurred her vision. What a terrible way for things to come out! She could not have foreseen . . .

Slowly she walked downstairs to wait for Joel; a whole life flitting before her mind's eye. Not her life, but Maggie's . . . On, on, the visions she couldn't stop of the child she could have had but had given away . . . The child who hated her now . . .

She was waiting for him when he came home. Waiting in the living room.

"Joel!"

As he finished placing his overcoat on the shaped, varnished wooden hanger and hung it among the other coats—his, Jeanette's, and yes, now Maggie's, in the long row in the entry closet—a premonition of disaster laid hold of him, causing him to move more slowly as he took off his scarf and draped it over a hook, adjusted his jacket collar, and closed the closet door.

Perhaps it was nothing, after all. But there was a quality in her voice that . . .

He looked at himself in the big gold-framed mirror that had hung there on the wall since before he was born. What became of past reflections? he wondered—feeling uncomfortably, as he sometimes did, that perhaps he was haunted by them. (Like past mistakes?) . . . The plump-cheeked little boy of whom so much had been expected; the babyish-looking prep-school kid who couldn't even catch a ball— or learn to swim; the oversized, overly handsome college boy who could never make decent grades. The young businessman, employed in his father's company, yearning to be ten years older, to be thirty-five and mature, so that he would know the answers. Thirty-five—ten years older but no wiser; only heavier by twenty pounds. Hoping his father would die soon, and *he'd* be head of Davis Manufacturing, with no one looking over his shoulder, criticizing, spewing out the words, *"Can't you ever get things right?"*

(But there always was someone looking over your shoulder, wasn't there. The directors of the company, or Roger Belden, or even his own subordinates in his own office. *Mr. Davis, you can't do it that way—it won't work.*)

"Joel!" she said again.

She was standing in the doorway to the living room.

"What is it, Jen?" He came close. Looked down at her.

"It's—Maggie." Her cheeks were scarlet, as though from too much rouge—but he knew she never wore it. (How beautiful she was!) "She telephoned a friend in Selkirk. I overheard her . . . Joel—she's quite sure the Mercedes— our Mercedes—was parked in front of the Weirs' house the afternoon Enid was shot. Maggie saw it there!"

Panic. He could feel it coming; tried to push it back.

"How would she remember? After all this time, she

couldn't possibly remember some car that might or might not have been parked—"

"She didn't remember just now: I gathered she told the police about it some time ago, and they didn't believe her. But now they might, don't you think? Given the identity of the car and our desire to get custody of Maggie—"

"Given nothing! How many gray Mercedes sedans do you suppose there are in this country? Hundreds! Hundreds!"

She frowned, and touched her fingers lightly to her forehead, as though the unpleasantness passing through it were making it ache. "With owners who had reason to get rid of Enid Weir?"

And he was back in Selkirk, parking the car, checking the street number, going up to the door of the long, handsome red brick house that belonged to the Weirs. If only he had never gone . . .

Sweat had started out on his forehead, and in the palms of his hands. "How can you accuse me, Jen—with nothing to go on! Nothing!"

She slumped and turned away and sank onto a chair. "I'm not accusing, I'm asking. I want to know what happened. Maggie thinks, of course, that *I* was the one who drove there, who killed her mo—well, she still calls Enid her mother, and probably always will."

He clutched—at what seemed to be at least a straw? "And was it you, Jeanette?" And was appalled, almost before the words had left his lips, to know that he was capable of making such a choice. And so quickly; automatically; before he'd thought.

Words rushed from him then, before the implication should reach her—that *sauve qui peut!* had come first to his mind, before any care for her. "You know, Jen, that you can count on me, *whatever* may have happened. You know that!" (Despicable! He loathed himself.)

The beautiful dark blue eyes narrowed; glittered. "Oh, no, Joel." She spoke softly, deliberately. "The day Enid was murdered you drove to Fort Wayne. On business. We both know that, don't we; because Roger asked you specifically, in case anything came up about it at the hearing. You got home sometime in the evening. And I know, and you know, that you took the Mercedes on that trip. I couldn't have used it that day."

The blood beat with a thrumming sound in his ears. Useless to deny what she said—he knew that. He hadn't thought it through when he'd been so quick to try to place *her* in Selkirk.

"And you could as easily have come through Selkirk on your return as not. Couldn't you. *Couldn't you!*"

He couldn't answer. Was totally incapable of saying yes or no.

She came to her feet and confronted him close up. "Joel, stop pretending you weren't there! Because I don't believe you. It's too late to play ostrich, don't you see? The mother of the little girl Maggie phoned is going to call Judge Owsler and tell him about the car; then she—the mother—is coming here to see Maggie, and me. The police will check now, as Roger didn't—in Fort Wayne. They'll find out what time your meeting there was over, what time you left . . ."

"It was an accident." The admission came out before he could stop it. Like floodwater bursting a dam. "Entirely an accident."

Her hands clenched tight into fists. "It *was* you!" (She had not been sure then, after all.) "When—just when, Joel, did you find out I'd had a child?"

So she'd tricked him into an admission; but then she'd always been able to manipulate him, do whatever she wanted with him . . .

When had he found out?

The bitter, dark look in Joel Davis's eyes was one of pity —for them both. "Did you actually imagine, Jeanette, that my father would let me marry you without having you investigated? I knew he wouldn't. I beat him to it—in case there was anything . . . And there was, of course; including what became of the baby. All in the report from the private investigator."

She was staring at him, amazed. He saw that this possibility had never occurred to her . . .

"I wanted you anyway; regardless. I paid the detective to make up a second report—incomplete—for my father. Leaving off the last part. Dad never found out."

Her brows drew together in puzzlement; in regret (for anguish suffered needlessly?). "Why didn't you tell me you knew? It would have saved me so much—" She seemed to have forgotten the present, and the murder of Enid Weir, as she looked back on the years that might have been different, at a marriage that was not quite as she had supposed it to be.

"I was afraid you'd be angry," he said. "And afraid my knowing would be a humiliation to you, and you'd hate me for it."

"Then why—"

"But lately—well, lately the lack of a child seemed to be turning you against me. I kept remembering that no adoption had taken place—according to the investigator's report. I wondered . . ."

"And so you went to see Enid Weir."

"Yes."

How well he remembered the middle-aged, rather unattractive face with its smallish eyes, fleshy nose, a long upper lip that drooped, a mouth defined in too-bright lipstick. No, he'd never be able to forget how Enid Weir had looked.

He said to Jeanette: "I thought I'd go unannounced; see the lay of the land before the Weirs could rig up a defense."

She'd understand, when he told her; she'd have to.

"My name's Joel Davis," he'd said—and had watched the slow dawning of fear, of hatred as the woman's mind moved ahead of the harmless-seeming words to latch onto the reason for his coming. And he had stepped past her into the foyer before she could stop him.

Enid Weir backed away from him, against the wall.

"Jeanette has no right! Nor you! She promised never—"

"My wife doesn't know I'm here. I came simply because I wanted to see her little girl—see for myself what she looks like." And that was all he'd meant to do, on his initial visit —size up the situation, get a look at Margaret. After all she might turn out to be an unattractive brat who could as well be left where she was.

But the low-keyed interview he'd planned seemed to escalate at once into something else.

"Maggie's not here. Not here, do you see?" Enid Weir's voice rose on a scale ascending toward hysteria. "And you're never coming near her! Never! Nor Jeanette! You tell her that!"

"I believe there was never a legal adoption, Mrs. Weir?"

Her face changed, when he said that; sagged, looked years older. But any pity he might have spared her was eclipsed by the gratification he felt in finding that he could act with such decisiveness. Mentally, he spit in Roger Belden's eye, at that moment. *See? If I were ever given the chance to do something myself!*

"I'm calling my husband! He's a lawyer, you know. He'll—"

She didn't say what he would do. Didn't know, probably —just hoped. Joel waited while she tried to reach him on the phone.

"He's not there," she said.

He wondered where Margaret was. She might come in any minute, he supposed. And finding Enid Weir's small, frightened eyes fixed on him, he wondered if she mightn't be thinking the same thing.

"If you'll wait just a moment, Mr. Davis." Her eyes flickered over him once more. "I'll be right back." She turned and hurried away down the hall.

It was then that he went on into the living room. If only

he'd *left* . . . He remembered standing there wishing he hadn't come. He couldn't handle scenes, they upset him too much. Why hadn't he known better than to walk into a situation like this? He wondered where she could have gone. To check on the child? To make sure she didn't come running in while he was present?

Quite suddenly he felt that he should get out of there; the warning message, materializing from thin air, was as definite as the sight of a coiled rattler, the smell of smoke, the sound of a stealthy footfall at one's back. Something subliminally perceived in the woman's behavior before she had gone off—

He turned too late to make an exit. She came toward him through the foyer; came into the living room, moving slowly, erratically. In her hand was a revolver.

"You're not to have Maggie," she said softly. "She's ours. I want you to understand that." She wiggled the gun, just slightly, keeping it pointed at him.

"Mrs. Weir!" he called out, in alarm.

"If you think I won't use it, you're wrong, Mr. Davis."

His hand moved upward in a protesting gesture, and the report as she fired was deafening. He didn't know whether he was hit, or how he came to be struggling with her; he only knew he was afraid as he had never been before in all his life. The gun was in his hand, then—but how he'd gotten possession of it he didn't remember; and although he was not conscious of squeezing the trigger, he was aware of wanting the awful screaming to stop, and it stopped, and it was after that that he remembered there had been a second report, which surprised him; he remembered it while he was watching, with astonishment, the strange, slow-motion effect of Enid Weir falling to the floor with the bullet wound in her forehead.

Afterward, he asked himself whether she had actually intended to hit him when she'd fired. Or whether she had even meant to fire? The whole thing might have been a bluff? But those were questions that would forever go unanswered.

He had left the Weir house, making himself walk calmly, deliberately, out to his car. He hadn't been able to think clearly about the revolver, so he'd taken it with him. Later, he had known he'd better get rid of it, and he wiped it clean with his handkerchief, and stopped at a bridge after he'd left town, and threw it over. Then he'd driven on—on and on for a long while. And had stopped somewhere along the highway for something to eat.

It took only seconds to live it again—as he'd done over and over, since that day. And he began, now, to tell Jeanette.

He hadn't wanted Jeanette to know, ever. But once she'd forced him to begin, the telling eased him; the sharing of the horror made it less. "I didn't *know* she'd do a thing like that. Her face was wild, with crazy eyes. She shot at me, and then I got the gun away from her, and it went off—and hit her." It would be all right, now. Not his fault, the accident; she'd *see* that . . .

But he was mistaken.

"You *fool!*" she shrilled. And the word was like a whiplash across his face; the first rebuke he'd received from her ever . . . ever. "Why, why didn't you get Roger Belden to handle everything for you from the first? *He'd* have known—"

The hurt was raw, but he tried to ignore it. He'd make her, *make* her, understand.

"For once in my life I wanted to do something *my* way." He spoke through clenched teeth. "I'm *tired* of asking someone, especially Roger, every time I blow my nose! Besides, I had no intention of saying anything about taking Maggie away from them. I only wanted to have a look at the child, and at the lay of the land. Don't you see?"

"Yes, I see—that you made a tragic mess of it. Why didn't you go to Roger *afterward*, then? You *said* it was an accident—"

"Go to Roger Belden with a thing like that? Oh, no!" But

she wouldn't understand. The years Roger had treated him as an incompetent; sneered while he told Joel Senior's son to do it this way, or that way. Jeanette didn't realize—(because he'd never told her; bad enough her seeing how his father—his own father—had made a nothing of him day after day as long as he lived) she didn't realize how Roger was always cutting the ground from under him just when he'd taken a firm stand, how Roger belittled him in front of the board of directors and made him feel a fool.

"You see what you've done, don't you?" She was breathing hard. He watched the rise and fall of her breasts. Never before had he seen her overtly angry; she was always so controlled, serene, and—perfect. "You've made a murder of an accident! You were *stupid!* You've ruined your life because you were stupid, and a fool!"

"Don't say that to me!" He could feel something inside him—it was like another person, with a mind of its own—taking charge. A person that was mostly anger, that saw things through a haze of red. This person was taking over, relieving the man Joel Davis of responsibility, of the necessity for thought. He felt relief; joy, almost—

The tears were running down her face. But even Joel Davis could see, as well as the other person did, that the tears were not for him but for herself. "I've tried all through our marriage to make a man of you; to prop you up, at least, so you'd look like one. But you haven't it in you. Poor spineless rich boy! You've made me waste my life on you. Why, you can't even beget a child! It's *your* fault, you see; you didn't know that, did you! You're *sterile! St—*"

It was a crystal ashtray that he brought down on her head —the other person, the one who was in charge.

But it was Joel Davis, Junior, who stood frozen in icy grief and despair, staring down at his wife lying unconscious with her head bleeding onto the white carpet.

Cinny had not been able to reach Judge Owsler. So she tried Orin Hogg. Surely someone you'd known back in high-school days . . .

"I'm sorry, Lieutenant Hogg isn't here. Can I help you?"

"Can't he be reached? It's urgent!"

"I'm sorry, ma'am, he's out on an emergency case."

She settled for leaving a message with the police sergeant; hoping that Orin would get it soon—and do something other than shrug it off? "Tell him I'm on my way to the Davis house in Indianapolis. I'll try to get Mrs. Davis to let me take Maggie Weir out of there on some pretext or other—for a visit, shopping, or something. I may not succeed. But the child can't be left there—not with this question unanswered, about the car. Tell him that!"

She left Trina to "mind the store."

"No, Trina, you'd better not come. I need you here. Call Maggie's Aunt Phyll, tell her what's happened, and see if she can find out where Judge Owsler is. Don't tell Aunt Lucille anything, if you can avoid it—it'd upset her too much. I've already told her I'm just going shopping."

Was this all a tempest in a teapot? she wondered as she went out the side door of Aunt Lucille's big old house and closed it after her. It could be, simply, that her natural anxiety concerning Gil's child, with Gil arrested now . . . But she broke into a run, as she neared the garage; time seemed of the greatest importance.

He was almost totally unnerved, on coming back into the room, to find that she had moved.

He'd been so sure he had killed her.

She lay face down, a body's length from where he'd left her. She'd been face up when he'd gone upstairs; crumpled in a heap.

The deep-piled carpet was dabbled and spotted and stained —awful, awful. He'd told her they shouldn't choose white, but she wouldn't listen.

In dread he felt of her. No pulse, no throb, that he could find. Turned her over. Dreaded to find her still breathing, still alive. Because the die was cast now. He'd done the thing for good and all when he'd struck her; he could never let her live to blame him, to accuse, to shriek, to scream. Or even just to look at him, knowing . . . knowing that he'd struck her—struck to kill.

A murder once started must be finished.

But he didn't see how he could possibly finish the job if it should prove necessary. How? How in the world? He rolled her onto the blanket he had brought. Peach-colored, the blanket. One of hers—he'd gone to her room especially to get it.

No slightest sign of life. And yet he'd better make sure. Keeping in mind the certainty that she was already fully dead made it easier to do; made it possible. He used the crystal ashtray a second time. The impact was sickening.

Chapter 12

"MR. DAVIS?" Cinny's mind had gone quite blank—of plans, of lines rehearsed.

"Yes—I'm Joel Davis." He was a ripely handsome man of about forty, and he looked, Cinny thought, as Joel Davis should look—expensively dressed in a chartreuse and brown plaid sport jacket, brown slacks. He was frowning slightly, trying to place her. (A friend of his wife's? Or someone he'd met at a party?)

"I'm Cynthia Howland," she said, smiling, trying to sound casual, at the same time looking past him into the splendor of a huge foyer with a curving staircase. Where, in this house, might Maggie be?

Her smile felt distinctly uncasual, but she went on. "My daughter and Maggie Weir are friends—"

"Oh." But the frown deepened on his face instead of going away.

"I'm in Indianapolis for some shopping, and I thought I'd stop in to see Maggie, if—"

"She isn't here."

"She isn't?" Her pulse was racing now and her mouth was dry and her lips felt stiff. "Oh, I see. Then I wonder if I could just talk to Mrs. Davis—your wife—for a minute."

"I'm sorry, she's not here either."

"Oh, dear!" And as the question, *Where can she be?* echoed back and forth in her head, she managed a little laugh that did sound right, a little distressed and rueful. "If

I could leave a message, then—may I come in? Just to—"

"Oh, of course!" He stepped back to let her enter. "Of course," he said in chagrin, and closed the door. "I apologize, leaving you standing there without even— You'll have to pardon my manners. As a matter of fact I'm rather upset. You see, I don't know where they've gone. Jeanette was expecting me home to lunch, and I came home and she isn't here." He ran a hand distractedly through dark hair which was already mussed as though he'd done this repeatedly. "And it's long past our usual lunchtime by now."

"You've no clue as to where . . . ? Something unexpected, I—"

"No clue at all. Her car's not in the garage, Maggie's not here, my wife left me no note . . ." He shook his head. "It's not like her."

The worried face she showed him was no fake. Had Maggie's phone call been overheard? Or her previous acquaintance with a gray Mercedes somehow wormed out of her? If Joel Davis had been elsewhere this morning, he'd know nothing of these things.

Yet he too was worried. Not like her, he'd said.

Something was very wrong. Must be.

"Oh, dear!" she said. "It's so worrisome when something like that happens. I mean—no note or anything . . ."

With a sudden rush of relief, she was convinced that the Davises' car could have had nothing to do with the murder. Maggie was mistaken; so many gray cars . . . On the drive down she had vacillated like this: first sure and then completely unsure that this whole thing was a wild goose chase.

But in that case there was no hope of clearing Gil . . . And her mind started on the same trip again, back to the certainty that Maggie was in danger, that she was in the custody of the woman who had killed Enid Weir. (She wouldn't harm her own child, surely? How many times in the last half hour had Cinny asked herself that question?)

She looked Joel Davis confidently in the eyes. "You know,

sometimes you can be *so* worried. And for nothing. There's always some perfectly logical explanation. I'm sure they'll be back any minute, or your wife will phone—"

He didn't smile, but some of his tenseness seemed to ease. "I'm sure you're right. Anyhow I'm sorry you've missed them."

"How is Maggie liking it here? I mean, you have a beautiful home and all, but she must feel quite strange as yet."

"Yes, I expect she does." And Cinny caught with his words a hint of something—antagonism? resentment?—something unexpected and at once disturbing. He didn't like the child his wife had brought into the house?

"I've talked very little with her," he added. "I've been—quite busy, and she's spent her time with my wife."

"Yes, I expect that's so." She watched him carefully now. "She's a wonderful girl—Maggie; we're very fond of her indeed."

"I'm sure you are. Well, if you'll excuse me, Mrs.—" He appeared to be about to edge her toward the door.

"If I can just write a little note for Maggie?"

He'd forgotten the request. "Oh. Oh, yes." Reluctantly. "Let me—I'm sure there's some paper . . ." He rummaged through the drawer of a gilt table beneath a huge gold-framed mirror.

She didn't help him. "I'm afraid I've no pen in my bag, or paper either." A lie, but it almost said itself.

"I'll find something. Be right back." He hurried from the foyer into the living room, and although it was clear he meant for her to wait where she was, she followed him.

"What a gorgeous house this is!" she exclaimed, as he half-turned in annoyance to find her tagging along, pushing herself in where she had not been invited.

He yanked open the drawer of a cabinet—in vicious haste. Slammed it shut and tried another. "I'm sure that somewhere . . ." A grating edge to his voice. No, he was not happy to have her here; couldn't wait for her to go.

"And a stunning living room!" she gushed, to fill the growingly angry silence. Indeed the room was spectacular. Except that the rug on which she stood was out of keeping with the rest. She glanced down at it—a rich, deep-toned oriental—and saw that it didn't belong here. The colors seemed dark and ugly against the white carpet; they should be on a wooden floor, where the reds and blues would gleam like jewels. Against the parquet, for instance—and as she glanced toward the stairway, a slightly paler rectangle of floor stood out, showing her the place from which the rug had been removed.

Why removed? When?

She had not met Jeanette Davis, but instinctively she knew that the lady of this house would never have put this rug in her white living room.

"Well, *finally!*" At last her unwilling host had found what he'd been hunting for. "Here. The best I can do." He smiled a little crookedly as he handed her a bridge scorepad and a thin gold pencil with a tassel on one end. She noted that he did not set foot upon the rug, but stopped at its edge.

It was placed peculiarly, too. The rug. Shoved almost into the corner by the—

It was fortunate that she had turned from him in search of a steady surface to write on—or her face would have given her away.

Surely he had not noticed, himself. Not yet. Before he did, she prayed she would be out of here; because he would realize at once that she couldn't have missed it in the all-white room . . . The pattern of bloody fingerprints on the wall, below an intercom panel . . .

Whose fingerprints?

And not only fingerprints. The reason for the rug's odd placement became to Cinny all at once sickeningly clear. Blood on a white carpet—perhaps a lot of it—would be quite a problem, wouldn't it.

No time to figure anything out; she knew only that she

must get away from here. Fast. If she could. Get help. Once Joel Davis became aware of what she'd seen—

"Now, what shall I tell her," she wondered aloud, falling back on the sort of brainless prattle any man would accept at face value from a female—and do his best not to listen to. Say anything inane, Cynthia; anything, and don't think about Maggie, really, or about blood, or injury, or death. "I just stopped in, you know, because I thought she might be homesick, and a familiar face—you know? Now where's something firm to write on—oh, the table in the foyer will do fine." And she managed to keep between Joel Davis and the telltale smudges on the wall as they strolled together back into the entry; at least *she* strolled, maneuvering carefully, and he progressed at her side in agitated jerks.

Oh, yes; his worry, and his distracted manner, when she'd arrived, had been quite genuine. But he had scarcely told her the whole of the truth! His wife and Maggie might well be missing. But—no message? No clue as to why Jeanette Davis wasn't here? *He* knew the rug had been moved. So he knew what was under it. He and Jeanette together, perhaps, had . . .

She wrote some kind of nonsense on the back of the score-paper, the while keeping up a running conversation about little girls, how wonderful they were, and sometimes so much trouble, but certainly worth it, oh, yes, you'll find that out I know now with Maggie here with you, yes indeed, tell her how sorry I was to miss her, and your wife too, of course we'll be meeting again because the girls are such good friends. On and on, one word right after another, so that he wouldn't be able, without being rude, to leave her side for a moment until she was out of the house.

Maggie. Where *was* Maggie? "Well, good-by, Mr. Davis. So nice meeting you." And out the door.

And the engine didn't kick over the first time, but the second try it did, and she was barreling down the drive across the huge yard—they must have a full city block, here, didn't they—do you no good to scream out of the windows of this house, probably, too far away for anyone to hear. And her legs felt like water, she was surprised she could press down on the accelerator.

Turned into the street and to the right, and turned then into the drive of the first house she came to in the next block.

Help. She must get help immediately. The police. Oh, this time they'd come! Blood. That was something concrete. You couldn't get more positive proof than that.

Out of the car door on her shaky legs, and up to the house —a cold, pretentious-looking place of dressed stone. Press the bell of a total stranger. Wondering whether Maggie (whole, injured, or dead?) was still inside the Davis mansion, or had indeed been taken off somewhere by Mrs. Davis.

Desperately she rang the bell a second time; a third.

No one home.

The houses were fairly close together; she left her car where it was and ran next door. Pushed the bell, battered on the heavy wood of the door and on the glass panels to either side. A big, beautiful house—Georgian. Red brick and white trim.

A window was opened above her and a head stuck out.

"The missus don't buy nothing from Avon!" a voice cried down, and as Cinny stepped backward to look up, the window closed.

"Oh!" Repeated ringing brought no response and, frantic now, she crossed the next yard, catching the fabric of her coat in some bushes on the way, tripping on the frozen ground by the drive and falling, cutting her knee on the crushed stone and ruining her pantyhose. And her nose was starting to run from the cold. She sniffed and made it to the door. A house very much like the last one—brick. Rang the bell, used the knocker . . .

The door opened. Oh, thank God. But only on a burglar chain.

"What do you want?" A slice of very elderly lady showing beyond the chain.

"I've got to call the police."

"Police? What for?"

"If you'll let me in. I can't explain out—"

"We don't let strangers in. Thieves've been all through here lately, broad daylight, some of them's nice-looking as you"—with a glance at her torn hose and bleeding knee—"why not, wearing stolen clothes? Furs, jewels—"

"Please! You call, then. Tell them the Davis house. Joel Davis. There are bloody fingerprints on the wall in the living room, and I think blood on the carpet under the rug. You'll call?"

"You're crazy, miss. Crazy." The door started to close and Cinny put her foot in it, an instinctive reaction, no doubt, passed down from some peddler ancestor, and useful now indeed. As the old lady leaned upon the door with all her wispy strength the pain in Cinny's foot was suddenly excruciating, and she jammed one end of her handbag into the crack to keep it open.

"You've *got* to call," she wailed. "You've *got* to! Tell them it's part of the Weir murder case in Selkirk."

All at once the pressure was off her foot and her bag. The embattled homeowner was no longer trying to close the door. "Oh, *that* one! That Selkirk woman? Mrs. Davis has the little girl . . ."

"Yes, *that* little girl! Please call. Tell them—'"

At last she made clear what was wanted, what must be done immediately. But still the woman would not admit her. "I'll call. I'm going to call right now." The door closed.

And will she? Cinny wondered. She thought so.

She picked her way, limping, back across the browned, frozen grass and the empty driveways, through the shrubbery

—the route by which she had come—trespassing all the way as she dredged up a Kleenex from her bag, for her running nose. Throw a rock, even now, through the window of the lady who didn't buy Avon products? Assure the police coming. As she pondered this question she caught sight, beyond the bare branches of the shrubbery along the Davises' property line, of a car moving along the drive she had come down in such haste a short time ago. A gray car, moving toward the street.

She broke into a run, and by the time the suspect vehicle had gained the street and again came into view, heading her way, she was crouched behind her car, watching through two layers of glass.

A gray Mercedes.

Impossible to determine, from this distance, whether there was a passenger with him. A sitting passenger, that is. A horizontal passenger, of course, would not be seen in any case; a thought that came to her unbidden as she got into her car.

Eddie, one of the sheriff's deputies, came into the little cell block. A stooped, gray-faced man, with more the air of a permanent convict than that of a jailer.

What now? Gil watched as he unlocked the cell door—Gil was the only one at present in detention—and the bars swung open.

"You c'n go," said Eddie.

"I can *go?*"

"Judge's waiting in the sheriff's office—he'll tell you. Brought over an order for your release. Judge Owsler."

Clem was indeed waiting. "Let's get you out of here," he said grimly.

"Yer things," said Eddie. He produced a list for Gil to sign and, opening the drawer of a battered green filing cabinet, began to take out the various items that had been impounded.

"Glad your sister-in-law finally located me, over at my daughter's house," said the Judge.

"*Phyllis?* She wants me *out* of here now? She should make up her mind!"

"And yer burglar tools," Eddie droned expressionlessly, "which was in the car you 'uz drivin'—"

The Judge looked around, somewhat startled.

"One chisel, one claw hammer, one flashlight, two *hairpins.*" The deputy cocked an eye at Gil and chewed silently and expectantly on his chewing gum, but was not rewarded with a comment of any kind. "And this . . ." With a flourish he drew what was clearly the *pièce de résistance* from the drawer, holding it by a tuft of hair, between thumb and forefinger. Patty's brother's wig. "Your disguise."

The Judge raised both eyebrows and seemed to shudder slightly.

"It's not mine," Gil said.

"It was right there, they tell me," Eddie insisted. "With yer other things, yer burglar—"

"Lent me by a well-meaning friend," he explained to Clem. And to its custodian, "I'll return it to her."

Eddie looked at it questioningly. "Looks like a 'his,' not a 'hers.'"

"Her brother's," Gil rasped, and signed for the lot.

"Did the paperwork myself, to get you out," the Judge told him; with a dubious glance at the paper bag in which Patty's oddments were again stowed.

"Have they arrested someone else, Clem? For Enid's murder?"

"Not yet. But some new developments—well, I've a feeling you'd better be on hand, not behind bars. And this—this—" He gestured at the little square of cells, and shook his head. "Actually you're out on bail, at my request; not usual in a murder case, as you know, but legally I can do it."

"Bail? Who's—"

"Phyllis Strothers has taken care of it."

"Phyll? My goodness." No time to wonder about such a change of heart. He was savoring the extravagant luxury of being able to put on his coat when he wanted and leave without hindrance. "Thanks, Eddie—for everything," he threw over his shoulder, and followed Judge Clement Owsler out of the sheriff's office.

"What's happened, then?" he asked.

"A lot."

Together they went down the steps of the jail.

"To begin with, your daughter found a gray car—and for God's sake, why didn't you bring it up at the custody hearing, Gil, when the child recognized her mother, and Mrs. Davis had to own up to a visit to Selkirk? This car that Maggie told the police she'd seen—"

"You mean Maggie's actually located it? The same one?"

"So she says. A gray Mercedes belonging to the Davises."

"The Davises!" As the full implication of this news reached him, Gil grabbed his tall, sallow companion by the sleeve of his overcoat. "Where *is* Maggie? She's not—"

"Don't know where she is."

"You mean—"

"Listen, Gil—everything's being done that can be. The police are fully involved at this point. And Orin Hogg can tell you more than I can." They were standing by Owsler's car, parked in a NO PARKING zone. "Here, get in. Unless you're touchy about going over to Police Headquarters after—" A quick, wry smile flitted over the Judge's face.

Gil got in, and Clem slid behind the steering wheel. They headed toward the City Building.

"But only this morning Orin told me he had checked on the cars the Davises owned. A rented car, maybe . . ."

"Well, in any case this gray car was in the Davis garage. What happened was that Maggie called a friend of hers here in Selkirk—what's her name? Daughter of that extraordinarily attractive girl you used to go with years ago. Cynthia Neiswanner. Anyway, Cynthia went tearing down to Indianapolis—after trying to get hold of me and of Orin Hogg. Apparently she did get into the Davis house, and out again, and alerted the Indianapolis police."

"And Maggie?"

Clem shook his head. "Don't know whether she saw Maggie, or what. Information's all very indirect."

Clem was holding something back. His set face, the slow, careful way he was speaking, told Gil he must be; there was something he hadn't gotten to yet.

And the short trip to the City Building seemed to be taking forever.

"What else, Clem? There's more, isn't there?"

Destination in sight. Clem Owsler slowed, brought the car to a stop spang in front of the building, in another NO PARKING zone.

"Seems someone called the Indianapolis police about there being blood all over, inside the Davis house . . ." He looked miserably over at his passenger.

"Oh, I see." He saw nothing, actually . . . He removed his numb, detached body from the seat of the car and stood it on its feet. "Thanks, Clem. Thanks. Talk to you later."

He hurried up the shallow City Building steps and through one of the glass doors into the building, and on along the wide corridor. All too soon—or was it not soon enough?—he would reach the always-open doors into Police Headquarters.

He tried not even to guess what he would learn there.

"Why won't you tell me where we're going?" she asked him.

But he didn't answer.

He wasn't even sure, himself, where he was going. He was still casting about in his memory of the nearby countryside for a suitable spot—and beginning fully to realize the enormous difficulty of the task that lay ahead of him.

He was worried, too, about the pale green Oldsmobile

he'd caught sight of in the traffic behind him. Car could belong to anyone—but it looked suspiciously like the one that woman, the mother of Maggie's friend, had been driving. Another complication?

This all still seemed incredible.

If only he could turn back the clock—change everything, make it come out differently. Today—especially today. His mind went back, trying, trying, to search out the exact moment when he might have altered the course of events. When? just when? But events had shaped themselves, irrevocably; he'd had no control over them.

He glanced covertly again at the child beside him on the seat of the car—the hated child. *Her* fault, all of this; if it weren't for her, none of it would have happened. What a pity he hadn't known, until they'd picked her up in Selkirk yesterday, how much he disliked children. He'd wanted one for Jeanette's sake, not his; he didn't know anything about children. And this one. He could hardly look at her without feeling guilty; without remembering the absolute horror of seeing Enid Weir falling, and lying there hideously dead on the floor. And now, of course, that dreadful double image, with the two bodies seeming to merge, to lie superimposed on the carpeting at his feet like something on twice-exposed color film. Jeanette—and Enid Weir. Jeanette—

The main requirement, he thought, was a high embankment off which he could push the car so that it would crash and burn. Not many high places in this part of the state. There were bridges over the rivers, but if he pushed the Mercedes off into the water it wouldn't burn—and he thought that a fire was essential.

Send it against a bridge abutment? But how could he aim it, when he wouldn't be in it, and be sure of what it would hit? It would have to be traveling at a good speed to have the right impact. And on level roads like these . . . Wouldn't do to have it veer off and stop itself harmlessly in a ditch. No way, no way at all, to explain the two bodies . . .

A highway overpass over the railroad?

Why not? The one up toward Marion had suddenly come to mind. He tried to remember what it looked like. A long, sweeping curve rising from the surrounding fields and passing over the tracks. It should be quite O.K. for his purpose.

If the car didn't burn, he'd set fire to it. And he realized how much better he would feel to have *her* burned. Instead of the way she was now. What he had done would seem a little less terrible if the evidence of it were charred away— the wounds, the matted hair. At least he hoped so.

He hadn't meant, ever, to harm her. But how could he help what he'd done in a blind rage?

He caught sight again, in the rearview mirror, of the green Oldsmobile—still trailing him far back. *If* that was Mrs.— what was her name? Holland?—she had not, then, rushed to a phone as he'd primed her to do, to set the police haring off after a mysteriously missing Mrs. Davis and the child she'd taken with her? Such a beautifully logical plan; fitting in so nicely with Maggie's disclosures to her friend. (As clever as anything Roger Belden could ever have thought up!) Because when he was finished with the car and it was found, later today, Maggie's suspicions of Jeanette, and of the role of the Mercedes in the Selkirk tragedy, would be clearly confirmed.

But if that was Mrs. Holland, following him . . . And this possibility was but one of the worries that beset him. The more he thought about the overpass business, the more apprehensive he became about the details. How could he stop and get Jeanette's body from the trunk and manage, unobserved, to put it behind the steering wheel? (Supposing, that is, he was not being tailed by the occupant of the Oldsmobile.) What if someone were watching? Visibility was marvelous on that stretch of road. And what should he do with

Maggie?

Tie her up and gag her, most likely. Whether Mrs. Holland had called the police or not, Maggie's long-distance call to Selkirk would have alerted a sufficient number of people to the probability of Jeanette's having killed Enid Weir; and so, in fear of discovery, Jeanette had . . . Yes, he would tie Maggie up.

He'd still have to get away from the scene himself. On foot. It would have to be on foot for quite a way, because he'd have to cut over to some other road. If he were picked up hitching near the tracks where the car had gone over, it would seem suspicious; whoever gave him a ride might remember him later and describe him to the police. Even though he'd thought to change to the right clothes—an old jacket, and scuffed shoes—he still might be identified.

If only he lived in California. Or the Allegheny Mountains. It was so simple, those cars containing bodies that were always being shoved over cliffs in movies, and caroming hundreds of feet down a mountainside and bursting into flames.

They were out of the city traffic now. Farms, through here. Too close together, though; he wished it were less populous.

People—in cars and trucks—everywhere. This was too well traveled a road. He felt crowded. Hemmed in.

He wished he didn't keep feeling so sick.

But at least he seemed to have lost the green Olds, he noticed. He could see a long way back, over the level highway. No sign of it.

He started as Maggie spoke. She hadn't said a word for miles. Not since the last time she'd asked him where they were going.

"Why didn't Jeanette come with us?"

He felt his face twitch, on the left side, in annoyance—or nervousness.

"Little girls aren't supposed to ask so many questions. But as a matter of fact, she'll—be with you later."

If only he had known, he thought again. If only he had known, before he'd decided to go to Selkirk and look in on Enid Weir, that he disliked children. He needn't have gone.

It had been only this fall that Jeanette had gotten around to talking about adoption. The idea had appalled him; he didn't want some stranger's child. But *her* child? That would be different, he'd thought. Why *not* the real thing, when she was right there in Selkirk? Little Margaret Weir.

Because without children, their marriage had been on the brink of ruin. How could he have known this, he wondered; have guessed how Jeanette felt, without making the full intuitive leap to the truth? The terrible truth that he was sterile. He'd seen something in her face, on occasion—an odd resentment, and, yes, a sort of repugnance that she must have tried to suppress. Repugnance at being married to a man whose seeming virility was a sham. *His* fault—*his.*

How she'd flung it at him—that final accusation—loaded with the resentment of years, telling him at last the thing she couldn't forgive him for! *You can't even beget a child! It's your fault, you see!* . . . And the accusation making of him a neutered thing—

The boy stared, incredulous, after the fast-accelerating Olds belonging to the lady who had handed him the ten-dollar bill.

Craziest thing that'd happened any time since he'd started work here. The ten, though, was pretty convincing, and as he walked past the row of pumps where his sole customer was having the tank of his car filled, he read the note the lady'd handed him:

KIDNAPPED CHILD, MARGARET WEIR, BEING ABDUCTED BY JOEL DAVIS IN GRAY MERCEDES, LICENSE #—

"Boy!" he exclaimed, breaking into a run, and feeling around already in his pocket for a dime for the payphone.

He understood the ten dollars now—it was not a tip, it was a reward. Would there be more, he wondered? Instantly visualizing himself astride the Honda whose ownership was his fondest dream.

"Operator? Get me the State Police. Fast."

"Listen," he said, when they answered on the second ring. "This is Lee Kelso, at Johnny's Mobil Station on Route Thirty-seven. A kid's being kidnapped. A lady stopped and handed me a note. She's following them. She gimme ten dollars, so it must be real . . ."

With a slow, horrid sinking feeling—nothing ever went right for him, did it?—Joel Davis realized that he was going to have to change his plan.

Far, far behind him on the highway running along here for miles between cornfields as level as a billiard table, he could see the pale green Oldsmobile coming along.

He'd been so sure, by now, that it wasn't her; that the whole idea was just a false alarm. But it must be Mrs. Holland. Maybe she had only dropped back, as a matter of caution.

Damn Mrs. Holland!

And it was at this point that he remembered the gravel pit.

He'd spotted it that other day, on the way back from Fort Wayne. He had cut over on a back road, from the route he would ordinarily have taken home to Indianapolis; cut over to go through Selkirk, for the ill-fated visit to Enid Weir. The quarrying operation he'd seen was abandoned—or had appeared to be; and he remembered just about where the place had been.

He brightened a little . . . Why, this was really better. No worry about working to set up the accident from the top of the overpass—having to get Jeanette's body out of the trunk and behind the wheel before someone came along on the road.

And this would work out better, too, because he'd have Mrs. Holland's car to get away in.

He began to plan.

There was an unusual feeling of tension in the Police Headquarters lobby—the big, square outer room that was the nerve center for the Department. Besides the duty officer there were two patrolmen, on their way out, who lingered, engrossed in what was coming in on the police radio that sat atop the long counter emitting crackles, beeps, and the flat, depersonalized sound of voices endlessly exchanging information. Orin Hogg had come out of his office, just beyond, and leaned in the doorway of the hall, half in, half out of the lobby, listening to the monotone voices. Gil was with him.

He had arrived to find Orin looking haggard with strain. "Maggie's all right, as far as I know," O.H. had said almost defensively to the man he'd worked so hard to indict for murder.

"What makes you think so? Clem says there's blood in the Davis house."

"I doubt that it's Maggie's. Presumably Cynthia Howland has seen her riding in a car with Joel Davis. Cynthia stopped and gave a gas-station attendant a note, and he called the State Police. They've got cars out now, looking for Davis. Or for Cynthia, who's apparently trailing him. Davis was heading northeast on Route Thirty-seven. This all came in on the hot line."

"Oh. What about the blood Clem said—"

"Just got the report on that a few minutes ago. The officers who went out to investigate broke in. There's fresh blood dripped all over one area of the living-room carpet, and it'd been covered up with a rug. Bloody fingerprints on the wall by an intercom system, as though someone tried to call for help. Whoever it was isn't anywhere in the house now; and this person is badly injured, they said—got to be."

At Gil's stricken look, he shook his head. "If it was Maggie, she wouldn't be sitting up in a car. Wouldn't be able to, that's pretty clear. Oh—and the investigating officers found sheets knotted together in the upstairs room that had been occupied by your daughter. She'd tried to get away. No sign up there that she'd been injured, or anything."

"I see. Just abducted."

"Well, she's still alive. And the State Police should catch up with Davis and your little girl any minute."

"Or Cynthia may, instead," Gil said grimly. O.H. didn't quite meet his glance.

Now as they waited, and there was no news, Orin turned and went back into his office. "Come on in." He slid into his chair, behind the desk. "Have a seat." Gil did.

O.H. tried to smile. "Cynthia's a regular female Double-O-Seven. She left me a message to get off my butt (not in those words)—about this gray Mercedes. Then she got in the Davis house somehow and got out. Gave some neighbor there instructions to call the police, and followed—God, this sounds like a T.V. episode, doesn't it?—followed the—uh—getaway car."

"Cinny was always pretty quick on the uptake. She shouldn't have had to do this, though." Gil's hands were clasped between his knees as he leaned forward—tense, waiting, agonized. If O.H. had only believed Maggie when she'd told him about the car. Yet he had checked, hadn't he?

As though reading the thought as it passed through his mind, O.H. said, "It was a company car. The Mercedes. I figured it had to be, when I got Cynthia's message this afternoon. I checked, and sure enough—it's registered to Davis Manufacturing Company. So—"

"Lieutenant—" The young officer who was on duty at the desk outside stood in the doorway. He looked awkwardly at Gil, then back at Hogg. "Just heard from them again. State Police can't locate either of those two cars—the ones on Thirty-seven. They say they must have turned off."

Gil asked the question. "Davis? And Mrs. Howland? Those the cars you mean?"

"Yes," Orin said heavily. "Those are the ones he means."

Why would he be going this way? Cinny wondered.

They had cut around Selkirk, to the northeast. Why in the world?

And where were the police? Surely the boy at the gas station . . .

They had left the main artery going toward Fort Wayne and were on a less-traveled road. Sort of doubling back?

She was afraid to get too close, yet it would be possible to lose him through here, because there were occasional patches of woods and he could turn at a crossroad if she were too far back. And so she closed in a little—rather perilously?

Long before they reached it, she saw the shape of the quarry. A gravel quarry, she thought—no longer in use. Filled in now with water.

She watched the Mercedes turn in on the overgrown dirt road, bouncing unevenly over the ruts and potholes. She hesitated. Surely it would be insane to follow him in.

Get help? She looked wildly around, and there wasn't a building in sight, save a fallen-down structure by the pit. There was no time to go for help. And she knew he had Maggie with him; she'd identified her, sitting in the passenger seat beside him, back when she'd been as close as she dared come in the Indianapolis traffic.

She decided. She turned in on the gravel-pit road, and stopped right there, left a handkerchief tied to the aerial, and followed on foot, at a run. If anyone should come by, her distress signal would be seen.

The distance she had still to go was farther than it had looked. And Joel Davis and Maggie were no longer in sight. He had pulled in behind the tumble-down shed; had disappeared between it and the remains of the quarrying equipment towering bleakly above, overhanging the scene like a gallows.

Her coat flapped open as she ran. There was a thin layer of ice, she saw, on the water in the pit. Nothing that wouldn't break the minute you stepped on it; nothing that would prevent an automobile from sinking promptly, with all it contained, to the bottom of an excavation it had taken years to make. A chilly, homemade burying ground.

She slowed to a walk as she rounded the corner of the old building; hesitated. There it was, the gray car. Through the roomy back window she could see them sitting inside—Davis and Maggie.

She walked to Maggie's door, tried to open it, but it was locked. Maggie at once opened it from the inside and slipped out of the car. Joel Davis did not seem to notice.

A thrill of tenderness coursed through her, and a wave of thankfulness, as her arm rested about Maggie's thin shoulder's; safe, for the moment—this frail-looking, vibrant child, Trina's friend. Gil's daughter, and hers, in the future? . . . Only a quick touch, and she signaled Maggie to run—run to save herself, for help, anything so long as she got out of here. Maggie hesitated. "Go on! Quick," Cinny framed almost silently with her lips, and Gil's daughter obeyed.

She herself leaned into the car on the passenger side, to say—to say what? His eyes turned to her—somber, dark, handsome; deep brown like the eyes of an animal. And then to her utter surprise he put his head down on his arms, which rested in a crossed position on the top of the steering wheel.

"I don't know what to do!" The plaint was low—desolate.

Without thought, Cinny slid into the seat beside him. Could she have been wrong? Perhaps he was no murderer at all—his wife had done something dreadful to herself and he was trying to cope . . .

"Where is she?" Cinny asked. "Your wife?"

"She's—I put her in the trunk. Wrapped in a blanket."

"Is she—"

"Oh, yes. She's dead. I made sure of it."

(Made sure whether she was? Or sure that she'd remain so?) Did one cluck with sympathy at this point, say, "There, there—?"

"How did it happen?" she asked softly.

"I hit her over the head with a crystal ashtray. Several times." He straightened up, faced her, looking stunned and bewildered. "She turned on me, you see, which wasn't like her. She'd always been on *my* side, never *against* me. I'd explained to her that it was an accident, completely an accident, Enid Weir being killed. Mrs. Weir fired at me, and I tried to get the revolver away from her, and somehow pulled the trigger. God knows my life's been a nightmare ever since, but I thought when I'd explained it carefully to Jeanette she'd see . . . But she didn't. She said I'd been a fool to go there, to try to handle it myself. She didn't understand that for once in my life I wanted to do something without Roger Belden telling me how. That I *couldn't* go to him for help afterward, not feeling—and she called me a double fool."

He spoke quietly and sadly, pouring out the story. And as Cinny listened, the feeling that "there, there," was what he really wanted from her grew stronger.

"Something rose up inside me, a kind of anger I'd never felt before, and it seemed to act for me without my having anything to do with it. *I* didn't want Jeanette dead—I only wanted her not to say those things, I wanted her to understand. And then, there she was—"

He broke off, staring into space, caught up in the re-enactment. And then, with no warning, Cinny found herself grabbed by the arm, as he looked disorientedly around at the broken ground, the stands of dried weedstalks, the iced surface of the water, and the rusting and rotting hulk of the old quarry screen and its conveyor system hunkered over them.

"Where'd she go? Where's Maggie?" His voice thick with alarm.

She felt the anger, the fear, in the crushing strength of his fingers. Even through her heavy coat.

How did you talk to a murderer? As you would to a sane man? or to a child?—or to a dangerous lunatic?

"She ran," Cinny said. "Just ran. I don't know where."

Gil and Orin Hogg, side by side, leaned over the edge of the communications desk, their eyes fixed on those of young Delbert Ogle, the duty officer. They were listening to his half of the telephone call that had come in.

It concerned Maggie.

"Your kid's O.K.," he told Gil as he hung up. But he at once turned away again to relay his information to the sheriff's office to which the call should apparently have gone in the first place.

Restlessly they listened to Delbert's half of *that*.

"Yeah . . . Yeah. Kid was picked up by a motorist—a woman—driving along Smith Road 'bout seven, eight mile outa town. Northeast . . . Yeah, northeast. They went on to a farm. Yount. That's the farm—Yount's . . . Listen, they need couple your deputies out there to look for this man Davis. And I'm sure the sheriff'll want to go. At the gravel pit—you know the place? That's where this Davis was when the little Weir girl got away from him. Mrs. Howland—that's Mrs. Cynthia Howland—she's with Davis. At the gravel pit . . ."

Gil's insides seemed to turn to a cold, sickening jelly.

A gravel pit? Cinny?

Delbert Ogle had hung up now. "I guess you heard?"

Gil nodded. "Maggie's all right?"

"Completely unhurt."

"But . . . Mrs. Howland. You don't know—"

"Don't know," he agreed. "She apparently followed Davis to the gravel pit and somehow enabled your little girl to get away. A man from the farm, where this lady called from, is on his way over to the place now—where Davis and Mrs. Howland were at. And the State Police oughta get there any

172

minute."

Gil turned to Orin. "Let's get out there."

"What good would that do? Chances are Davis isn't even there by this time. Any minute we'll hear—"

"If you don't want to go, *I* will!"

"Don't. Have a little patience, Gil. We should learn more any minute; if you go out there in your car, you won't know what's going on, or where anyone is, without the police radio. Besides, I believe someone's bringing your daughter here— isn't that what I heard you say, Del?"

Delbert Ogle, neat and skinny in his uniform, nodded. "Lady who picked her up in the first place. Bringing her right here to her dad. I told her she might as well."

"See?" said Orin.

Gil started to argue, then thought better of it; sagged against the counter. "I suppose you're right—at the moment."

"Your *borrowed* car, I meant," Orin amended. "I noticed that someone named Patricia had lent it to you?" He lifted an eyebrow, and Gil could see the term *womanizer* going through that hard red head again.

Gil eyed O.H. reproachfully. "It belongs to Fred Towse's intended—very nice girl he's going to marry as soon as he gets his divorce." Incredible that with life and death—Cinny's—hanging, perhaps at this moment, in the balance, he could talk of other things: the future, people getting married. But that was the only way one survived . . . Keep talking, force yourself to swallow, to breathe, to wait, to have confidence in tomorrow, next week, next year.

"Well, it's still parked in the official lot with the patrol cars, where it was put when we impounded it—in case you want it."

"Thanks for telling me. But you're right, of course—I'd better hold on here. For now." A gravel pit. He couldn't think of anything worse. And actually there was nothing he could do—that was what made it so much worse: the helpless, timeless, ubiquitous, overwhelming feeling of frustration, of being able to do nothing at all. Even if he went out there it would still be too late, he couldn't make it in time because by now, if Davis were going to, he would already have—and someone else was going; had gone: a man from a farm. Maybe the man already knew; had gotten there and had found her—or had not found her?

How long before they would hear? How long before he would know? Cinny, a smiling girl in a white evening dress, the girl of his choice, with the whole future stretching away before them. The terrible letter, the icy shock, *I'm going to marry Ted Howland.* A world of bitterness—but not like this; no, not like this—something he'd gotten over, more or less. But this—this never came again. The long-ago past becoming again, incredibly, your present, your future . . Cinny in his arms, out at the Fenton place, as if two decades and more had not gone by . . . All those past times, years ago, binding them together again now—

And then there was word.

A State Trooper had reached the scene, called in a report. There had been no one at the quarry, on his arrival, except the farmer, who said there had been no one there when he had come—only a car, registered to Mrs. Cynthia Howland, with a distress signal fluttering from the aerial—a handkerchief. And whether anyone or anything had gone through the ice on the water and sunk to the bottom of the pit could not be determined. There was a place where the ice was broken through. Boys playing, or a dog—anything could have made a hole there. But because of the hardness of the ground, frozen solid along the quarry rim, there was no telling who might have stood there today—kids, a man, a woman . . . no telling.

"Oh, my God!" said Gil, mostly to himself.

"This Davis is armed." The announcement, coming over the police frequency in an impersonal, metallic voice, cut into Gil's consciousness with the sharpness and pain of a knife

"Got that? Armed and dangerous. He's carrying a handgun."
All the officers hunting down Joel Davis were being warned.
But Cinny? Drowned or shot, either way she . . .

They had driven first one way and then another, as he hunted for Maggie—both of them searching, as if together, for a lost child about whom they were desperately anxious. Cinny had to remind herself, once or twice, that his anxiety stemmed from another cause than hers; that their hopes were opposite—his to find her (search and destroy), while hers was that nowhere would they see the movement of a smallish figure on the road ahead of them, or catch a glimpse of a navy coat against the drab winter-dead fields to either side.

She had felt little surprise, on her own account, that he had not killed her and sunk her in the quarry as she was sure had been his intention; he hadn't the time, once he'd missed Maggie. Whatever he did with Cinny would have to be later on. She even had the impression that he thought she was helping him in his search—that if she sighted the escapee she might give away the fact by some involuntary sound or gesture. And so she steeled herself not to.

"You're not going to find her," she said at last. "I think you can assume by now she's gotten word to the police."

"No! She mustn't be allowed—"

"You're lucky if she has. Because that should stop you before you make things worse for yourself. Don't you see? If you go *now* to the police—"

"Oh, no! No."

"The matter of premeditation makes quite a difference in how you would be charged. Surely you know that. You told me Enid Weir's death was an accident: manslaughter, then. And the other—there was no intention; you said that and *I* believe you. Something done in a sudden blind rage—"

"Yes, that's what it was. Blind rage." Slowly he was bringing the car to a stop on a long stretch of road dividing barren fields devoid of any human presence. A pair of heavy-footed bay farm horses stood or wandered about in the next field but one, up ahead. The ground on the right sloped down to the river, which she could place by the trees along its banks; it ran along at the back of the row of fields. Water again. She shivered. A lane between the fields went down in that direction.

"If you gave yourself up now," she persisted, "the charge would be at worst second degree. Possibly even manslaughter for both."

He turned and looked at her. And he appeared to be quite rational. "Did you call the police, after you came to the house?"

Ah, the crucial question. How to answer it. With the truth, pressuring him further to give himself up? Or would it only send him into another blind rage and scotch all hope of her coming out of this?

Safer to lie, and play for time.

But Cinny lied poorly—when forced to—and she knew it.

"Yes, I phoned them." By proxy, she had; the same thing.

His hands tightened, flexed, and tightened again on the steering wheel. "What did you tell them? That Jeanette was missing with the child?"

Her brain seemed paralyzed; unable to frame any answer but the truth.

"No." In a husky, accusing voice. "I told them there were bloody fingerprints on the wall, and blood on the carpet. They'll have been to the house by now, and seen them."

He sat on behind the wheel, not looking at her—instead watching one of the horses, the one with a white foot, which had walked toward them as far as it was able and was staring over the fence toward the Mercedes. Crows cawed and flapped back and forth in the trees by the river, and a pale sun struggled without success to burn its way through the gray overcast, silvering a heavy bank of cloud. She wondered where Maggie was.

"You can't undo any of it, you know," she said. "Nor

pretend it didn't happen. It's too late for that. They're waiting for you now, at your house. The police. You can't blame Enid Weir's death on your wife anymore; that didn't work out. Don't you see? All you can do, Mr. Davis, is to go to the police and give yourself up."

She thought he hadn't heard; was perhaps beyond reach. Then, almost imperceptibly, he nodded.

"Will you drive?" he asked her. "I—can't, anymore."

"I'll be glad to."

They changed places. He got out and she slid over while he went around the front of the car. There were several seconds when she could have gotten away, could have put the idling engine in gear and left him there and driven to safety. But she didn't. She couldn't have; it didn't seem a decent thing to do.

He got in. Settled himself in the seat beside her. Reaching over, he took something from the floor beneath her seat; stuck it in the pocket of his windbreaker. A handgun of some sort, she realized suddenly. And knew she should have driven off and left him when she'd had the chance.

She pulled into the little lane between the fields and backed around, to return the way they had come. She wasn't sure she could drive either, but found that she could.

She accelerated down the straight, blacktopped road; terribly aware of him, sitting there hunched in his seat, his life in ruins.

"I'm not like that, you know," he volunteered after a while.

"I'm sure you're not. Sometimes things just go wrong."

"Yes, they do."

But if he wasn't like that, what was he like? *Something rose up inside me . . . seemed to act without my having anything to do with it.* Could he be schizophrenic? Two people, one mild and one violent? Like William Heirens, in Chicago, back in the forties—the classic case of split personality. William, the scholar, the model youth—and his alter ego, wild and daring George Murmans. William, as George, had committed the very real crimes of his imaginary friend. And had not known, it had seemed.

So Joel Davis had not wanted his wife dead, and yet—

Best not to think about that angle of things.

And there was a long ride yet ahead of them, because he quite soon said, "I want to go directly to the police. No calling from someplace and waiting—I couldn't do that. I wouldn't wait."

"All right."

And would they make it all the way to the police? Without his changing his mind? Or bashing her head in on the way?

And again she wondered just how you talked to a murderer. And what about. Do you generally go South in the winter, Mr. Davis? Florida, or do you prefer the Caribbean? Really? I suppose so. My husband used to like Bermuda, when he was alive. No, oh, no—he died a natural death. No blow to the skull, nothing like that, just a simple heart attack. If you're going to go, it's the best way . . .

Actually she said nothing, for fear of deflecting him from his intention. His *present* intention, anyhow, of going to the police.

While they were waiting, Gil had thought of Trina. He phoned.

"Mr. Weir—I don't know where Mom can be all this time—"

He told her. Some of it. "I'm sure she'll turn up any minute." He tried to believe it. Couldn't. Did. *But where was she?*

He did the best he could to sound calm, assured. "I'm waiting at Police Headquarters for Maggie. If your mother . . ."

"Can't I come and wait with you?" The voice thin with fear, sounding not a day over eight.

"Well, I'm not sure—"

A rush of words. "But I can walk there, it's not far at all, Mom lets me walk downtown all the time. And I'm not supposed to tell Aunt Lucille, because she mustn't worry. But she'll wake up soon from her nap—*Please,* can I? I'll leave her a note. Aunt Lucille . . ."

And so when Maggie came flying up the steps of the City Building and into Police Headquarters in search of her father, Trina Howland was with him, waiting in the Headquarters lobby.

"Oh, Trina! You should have been there! I was locked *in,* and then *kidnapped,* and—Daddy, they said you're not arrested anymore?"

"No. Thanks to your efforts, I'm not arrested anymore." Holding tight to her, Gil smiled over her head at the woman who had followed her in. "You're Mrs.—?" and he tried to thank the stranger, a plump, pleasant-looking brunette who kept saying it was nothing, nothing at all, she had six children herself, mostly girls.

Euphoria enfolded Maggie. She was safe; restored to her father—whom she, Maggie Weir, had saved singlehandedly, like a heroine in a book! . . . And then recollection claimed her. She looked soberly at her best friend, feeling at this moment so horribly lucky by comparison. Trina—all Trina *had* was her mother.

"Trina, I'm sure she's all right. They'll get to her any minute. There are tons of people looking for them out there where we were, police cars and everything . . ." But the clear, almond-shaped eyes of her friend looked only worried, not reassured. Scared. Very scared.

The mother of six left, and Maggie squeezed into a wide-seated Police Department chair beside Trina, with an arm around her.

"Maggie?" Lieutenant Hogg bent over her. "I'd like you to tell us what happened—your father and me. If you think you can . . ."

And so the three of them went into his office, leaving Trina Howland sitting alone, pale as an invalid, waiting for word of her mother.

The lieutenant asked the questions; Maggie's father listened.

"Where was Mrs. Howland when you left her?"

"She was just getting into the car with Joel—Mr. Davis."

"Did he force her to get in?"

She shook her head, and told them about Mr. Davis just sitting there, like he'd forgotten where he was or something, and how she hadn't wanted to leave Mrs. Howland.

"But I knew she wanted me to get help, and I'd better go while I could. Because he had a gun, under the seat. He showed it to me."

Her father gave a heavy sigh and bent his head, and she thought of how sure she and Trina were that they still cared about each other—her father and Mrs. Howland.

"I wondered," said the lieutenant to her father, "how they knew he was armed. You told one of the officers, did you, Maggie?"

"Yes. The one who came to the farm. He asked me."

The big redheaded policeman was scowling. "Do you know, Maggie, what's become of Mrs. Davis?"

"I think she's—she's dead." And she told them.

The voice had startled her, coming from the little speaker in the wall. It had been a while after her blood-mother had locked her in and gone away.

"Maggie? Lis—listen to me, darling." The voice muddied, somehow—almost drunken. "You must try . . . get away. Try . . . Sorry—sorry I—locked you in." The unmistakable urgency of the message, and something odd about the breathing Maggie could hear in the electronic silence of the connection had caused a tingle of fear to spread all through her.

"He'll kill you, I . . . think. Afraid—" The voice had broken off.

"Jeanette—" She'd tried to call her back but got no answer. There'd been footsteps in the hall, then, and after that the sound of someone running water—she could hear it through the pipes in her private bathroom. Joel? . . . And